Playing with Fire
A Jed McCain Mystery

Bill Cronin

Copyright

Printed in the United States of America

ISBN 978-0-9908381-7-3

Library of Congress Cataloging In-Publication Data
Library of Congress Control Number
2018900236

Dedication

To Linda

Acknowledgements

With special thanks to Mike Lanfersiek of Orlando, a retired officer with the Florida Department of Law Enforcement, for his valuable insight.

Thanks also to Larry Lott, New Smyrna Beach, expert in all things outdoors, for his tour and background about Disappearing Island.

1

John Hammond shoved his twenty-two-foot Boston Whaler away from his dock behind his three-million-dollar home that backed onto the Indian River. To his south, the North Causeway Drawbridge connected the beachside and the mainland of Coronado Beach. The bridge was elevated, waiting for a tall sailboat to pass. Hammond moved into the river and, once in the channel, turned north.

It was six-fifteen a.m., and Hammond was running late. An offshore wind pushed smoke from a western inland brush fire across the mouth of the inlet and out to sea. Hammond wanted to photograph the Ponce Inlet Lighthouse just as the sun broke the horizon. He hoped the smoke between the lighthouse and the sun would diffuse the light to create an orange and red backdrop for a silhouette of the lighthouse. A rare confluence of elements, he predicted, would create an award-winning image.

With green channel markers to port, he glided past multi-million-dollar homes on the east side of the channel wedged up against the river. Docks of various lengths extended like fingers into the channel. Yachts, sailboats and offshore fishing boats spoke to the wealth of the home's occupants. He navigated around a mangrove island as he moved into a wide bay at the mouth of the inlet and opened the throttle. The current, nearing high tide, was strong. In the backwater of the inlet, there were several sandbar islands formed by movement of sand by tides in and out of the inlet. The incoming tide submerged most of them. The largest of these islands the locals had named Disappearing Island. It was a popular spot for local boaters who used the island as a private beach. Historically, Disappearing Island had been underwater at high tide, but a recent hurricane had piled enough sand on it that a narrow strip of land survived the tide. At six thirty a.m., there was seldom anyone on the island.

Approaching Disappearing Island, Hammond noticed something floating in the water. As the sun breached the horizon, he gave the object a second look. It appeared to be a human body floating face up. He cut the throttle, turned hard to port and drifted closer to the island. Only a sliver of sand perhaps fifty feet wide by several hundred feet in length remained above the surface. A well-endowed woman of slight build floated in the water, her head resting on the sand. The wake from Hammond's boat as it angled closer almost dislodged the body from shore.

Hammond nudged the sandbar, jumped from the boat and approached the body. The woman appeared to be in her late twenties to early thirties. He could tell from the milky appearance of her blue eyes that she was dead. He bent over and felt her left wrist for a pulse, but there was none. The woman had bleached blond hair and wore tan mid-thigh shorts, an untucked white sleeveless blouse and no shoes. He saw no signs of violence. Other than her shriveled skin and clouded-over death stare, she looked as peaceful as the sunbathers who'd flock to the island later that day to enjoy the sun, the sand and the cool water washing through the inlet.

Hammond pulled his cellphone out of his pocket and dialed 911. As best he could, he gave the dispatcher his location, instructing them that they could only reach his location by boat. He agreed to wait for local police or the sheriff's deputy to arrive. He knew that the rising tide would soon free the body from the island. He reached into his boat, pulled out his camera and took several pictures of how he'd found the body. Then he stepped behind the dead woman, lifted her by her shoulders and pulled her up on what remained of the island. He turned toward the east; the sun had cleared the horizon as a deep red fireball, one of the most beautiful sunrises he had ever seen. He took several shots, but without a subject in the foreground, it lacked character, perspective and focus. He put the camera back into the boat and prayed the phenomenon would recur the next morning.

2

I was up before six in the morning. I made a pot of coffee and opened the sliding glass door from my small eat-in kitchen to my back yard. With coffee in hand, I walked out to my dock, which backed onto the Indian River, and waited for the sun to come up. This was my routine most mornings, and the most peaceful part of my day. Since becoming chief six months earlier, I prized this private time separating me from the insanity of my work. The water lapping up against the pilings of the dock, the repetitive screech of the sea birds, the boats rocking in their moorings at my neighbor's dock and the ever-present breeze that meandered down the Indian River all contributed to the calm with which I began my day.

As I placed my cup on the bench and sat down, the air, normally filled with the odors of fish and salt, smelled of smoke. It had been six months since the Night Fire Strangler had killed Sarah James. Mourning her loss had been difficult. First, she'd been my boss with the NYPD before I'd retired as a twenty-year veteran and homicide detective. She had been responsible for getting me my current job with the Coronado Beach Police Department. I had been in love with her and felt I could have done more to prevent her death.

Sarah had left the NYPD before I did and landed a job with the Florida Department of Law Enforcement. The Night Fire Strangler had followed me from New York to Florida and resumed killing women in ritualistic fashion from my first day on the job. Sarah had offered her help and that of the FDLE to help me find the killer. Sarah had been the Strangler's final victim. I'd killed him within minutes of him ending Sarah's life.

The wounds of her loss were healing, but on some days, they felt as fresh as the day I'd lost her. The feelings of guilt that I could have done more haunted me, something I knew I'd live with for the rest of my life.

This morning, my mind was filled with pressing matters.

My neighbor, AJ McFarland, was the city's new mayor. In his seventies, AJ had lost his wife to cancer and had been a significant source of strength and support as I grieved Sarah's loss. Thirty years my senior, AJ was fascinated with the PD. We would sit together on my dock, and he would probe into the workings of the department and major cases we were working on. Despite my repeated refusals to discuss open investigations with him, he was relentless in asking.

Neil Jarret, the city manager, had hired me with the understanding I'd follow chain of command with respect to my communications with the mayor and city council, and had warned me that violations would be grounds for my dismissal. The previous chief had developed personal relationships with the mayor and several council members and ignored Jarret regarding department matters that came before the council. Although I assured him I didn't and wouldn't discuss PD business with the mayor unless it was in Jarret's company, he felt that my friendship with the mayor and AJ's aggressive lobbying on the PD's behalf made his job as city manager impossible.

After Sarah James' death, and before I'd realized how aggressive AJ could be once he grabbed onto something, I had casually mentioned to him my desire to form our own crime scene investigation unit and crime

5

lab. I hadn't mentioned this to Jarret before AJ blindsided him with it in a city council meeting a month ago. On major crimes, the FDLE handled all crime scene investigation for the Coronado Beach PD. Before Jarret realized what was going on, AJ had made a motion and the council had approved a committee, including me, to develop a plan and budget to bring crime scene investigation in-house.

Jarret was livid. I was, too. AJ had scheduled the committee's first meeting for that evening. Jarret had seethed and demanded we meet in his office this morning to discuss it.

Before I'd left the PD the night before, Sergeant Martha Johnson, my assistant, had met with me regarding her son and only child, Deshon. He was seventeen and had involved himself in a juvenile gang in Daytona. Deshon's father had left the scene when he was an infant, and Johnson had raised the boy as a single parent with sporadic and ineffective help from her parents, who lived in Deland. She'd asked me to meet with Deshon and try to talk some sense into him. I met the boy at the PD Christmas party when he came to pick up his mother. He'd seemed like a nice kid, bright and confident.

I found the job of chief had little to do with preventing or solving crime. I spent most of my time dealing with personnel issues, the politics of policing in the community, coordinating with other PDs and law enforcement agencies in the surrounding counties and trying to keep a lid on the frequent controversies between the city council and city management.

One of the jobs I hadn't given up was investigating major crimes, despite my assurances to Lieutenant Leslie Downs, head of investigations for the department, that I'd turn these duties over to her and her unit. The previous chief had excluded her from investigating major crimes, preferring to have the FDLE handle them. When I'd became chief, to prevent Downs from leaving the department, I'd committed to her that her unit would investigate major crimes in the future. The reality was that Downs, and her team helped me with those investigations. I used the excuse that she needed more training and time before she was ready for that role. She and I both knew it was a cover to keep my hand in the only part of the chief's job I enjoyed. Although Downs kept after me to let that responsibility fall to her and her unit, we had significant chemistry on the job, and I thought she enjoyed the opportunities we had to work together. She'd never said that to me. Perhaps this was more of a hope on my part than fact.

I turned to catch the red sun as it rose over the roof of my home. I heard my cellphone ring on the table in the kitchen, and I sprinted from the dock to the house to answer it.

"McCain," I said, out of breath.

It was Leslie Downs. "We have a floater on Disappearing Island. A woman. A boater found her a few minutes ago."

"That's out in the Indian River, isn't it? Near the inlet?"

"I'm at the city marina. The boys are fueling the boat. How soon can you get here?"

I looked out the sliding glass door northwest across the Indian River and could see the marina. "Ten minutes."

I parked my unmarked cruiser in the PD parking lot and ran across the street, past the ruins of Turnbull Mansion in Old Fort Park and to the marina. Downs and a uniformed officer were in the boat with the outboard idling. I stepped onto the bow, Downs cast off the line and the corporal, standing at the console, backed the twenty-foot open boat into the channel and moved into the Indian River. At a little better than idle speed, we passed under the North Causeway Drawbridge and cruised toward Ponce Inlet. Out in the open, off the port side, a plume of smoke was visible out to the west; the fifteen-knot wind would no doubt hinder efforts to bring the blaze under control.

As we approached the inlet, there was a boat similar in size and design to the PD's anchored at Disappearing Island; a man signaled for our attention. The corporal eased back on the throttle, drifted alongside the waiting craft and nudged into the sandbar. It was then I noticed the woman's body lying on what remained of the sand.

"Hi. John Hammond," the man said. "The tide was coming in, and I didn't know what to do. If I didn't pull her onto the sandbar, she would have floated out into the inlet, and I didn't want to disturb the body any more than I already had."

"Not to worry," I said. "You did the right thing. Where was the body when you found it?"

"I was here at sunrise. Then, her head was resting on the sand, but with the rising tide, the rest of her body was afloat in the water."

Downs had already pulled a notepad from her pocket and began to take notes.

I asked, "What time did you find her?"

"Six-thirty. I took some pictures of where I found the body." Hammond picked up his digital camera, turned it on, opened the picture and handed me the camera. "I called 911 right away."

"May we keep your camera until we can download the pictures?"

"That's a very expensive camera Mr..."

"Chief McCain but call me Jed."

Downs reached for the camera. "We'll take good care of it."

I stepped out of the boat onto the sandbar. Downs did the same. Kneeling next to the body, I began with the woman's toes and worked my way to her head, looking for signs of trauma, violence or any other clue that would explain her death. None was apparent. The wrinkled appearance of her skin indicated she'd been in the water for a while, but her milky eyes showed no signs of petechial hemorrhaging, which would show drowning or strangulation. Other than a slight pinkish appearance of her skin as it grayed from lack of blood flow, there was nothing to hint at the cause of death.

I asked Hammond, "Did you find any identification or anything else on or near the body?"

"No. Can I leave now?"

"You'll have to wait for the crime scene folks. You touched the body, so we will need your prints. They'll have more questions about where and how you found the body. We'll let you go just as soon as we can."

Downs asked, "What do you want to do with the body?"

"Do you have a bag on the boat?"

Downs looked at the corporal, who nodded.

"It appears we do," Downs said.

I said to Downs, "Let's bag her up and put her on the boat. Since the body was afloat in the water and Hammond pulled her up onto the island, it is no longer in situ. This will save the M.E. having to make the trip out here. Call Hunter and have him meet us at the marina.

Call Agent Torres and have her crime scene crew meet us there, too. They can use this boat to come back here and do their thing. I don't know what, if anything, they'll find."

Downs called medical examiner Damon Hunter and Agent Alicia Torres, FDLE's crime scene supervisor. "They'll be at the marina when we get there."

Before we placed the body in the bag, Downs made one final inspection of the decedent. She opened the mouth and smelled the open cavity. She then rolled the body face down and scrutinized her from head to foot.

"All right, let's lift her onto the bag," she said.

We unzipped the black body bag and lifted the woman into it. With the corporal's help, we lifted the body over the side of the PD boat and onto the fiberglass deck.

"When you smelled her breath, was there any sign of alcohol?" I asked Downs.

"None," she said. "Why don't you ride back to the marina with the body, and I'll stay here and keep Mr. Hammond company until Torres and her crew arrive. I'd like to be here until they finish. We're going to need some divers out here, too. I doubt they'll find anything, but it's a stone we need to turn over."

At the Coronado Beach Marina, the M.E. parked his van behind the PD's boat slip and stood waiting with his arms folded across his chest. As the corporal nudged the boat against the dock, Damon Hunter dropped into the boat.

"Jed."

"Doc."

"What do you have for me?" he asked, but before I could answer, he bent over the body and unzipped the bag. He placed a thermometer in the dead woman's armpit and began a thorough investigation of the body.

"She was floating near Disappearing Island. In fact, I think someone dropped her on the island before the tide came in. A boater found her at sunrise. I looked at the body over at the scene, but I didn't see anything. There was a slight pinkish color to her skin, but it doesn't appear to be there now."

Hunter said, "No signs of trauma." He smelled her opened mouth as Downs had done. "No alcohol." He pulled out the thermometer. "Body temp indicates time of death was six to eight hours ago. My best guess is between ten and midnight. I agree, there aren't any signs of violence." He turned the body over to examine the back. "I won't be able to tell you much until I get her back to the shop."

"Natural causes?" I asked.

"You found her on a sandbar in the middle of the inlet floating in the water. That's about as natural as steak Diane at McDonalds."

"Yes, there's that. Any signs of drowning?"

"None that I can see. You say there was a pinkish tinge to her skin at the scene?"

"Yeah, but I don't see it now. Did her breath smell of almonds?"

"You are thinking cyanide?" Hunter bent over the woman's head, opened her mouth and sniffed several times. "I don't smell anything, but if it was cyanide, the aftereffects dissipate quickly."

I asked, "Tox screen?"

"I'd do one regardless, given the suspicious circumstances, but I'll look specifically for cyanide. Perhaps there will still be traces in her organs, but don't count on it. As soon as I have something, I'll be in touch."

The tall, gaunt man with thinning hair zipped up the blond woman with blue eyes in the bag. Hunter's assistant wheeled a gurney onto the dock next to the boat. Hunter, his assistant and I lifted the body out of the boat and onto the gurney, and the M.E. wheeled the body away. As the ME's van left, Alicia Torres pulled up in an FDLE crime scene van, accompanied by two other techs.

Alicia Torres jumped from the driver's seat, walked around the front and dropped onto the dock. She was in her mid-thirties and had a fair complexion, pale green eyes and long light-brown hair she wore up and under an FDLE baseball cap. She wore a black overall-like uniform.

"McCain.". "We received a call that you found a body?"

"The M.E. just left with her. We need you to go out to the place where they found her. A boater named Hammond found the body. He's there with Lieutenant Downs. There's not much of a scene to examine. The body was dropped on a sandbar that's now almost submerged."

"Downs called me. I have a diver coming. He should be here in a minute."

"The corporal will take you and your team out when the diver arrives. I'd like you to question the boater first, get all the information he has, which isn't much, and kick him loose. He's been out there for a while waiting on us."

"All right." Torres looked in one direction, then another, and moved closer to me. "Could we have a private word?"

I nodded and followed Torres a few steps away from her team.

"What's up?"

"I heard you're thinking about setting up your own crime scene unit."

"Where did you hear that?"

"In the newspaper."

I said, "Oh, the city council meeting."

"Well, is it true or not?"

Torres was attractive, a foot shorter than me, but she had a demeanor that made me feel she was looking me straight in the eye.

"We're discussing it. Nothing more than that. Why? Are you interested?"

"Yes... Well, it depends."

"Money?"

"Yes. The state's pay scale sucks. Great retirement, but it's hard to make ends meet on what they pay."

"What about Jim Cahill? I don't want to create a problem with him." Jim Cahill was the special agent in charge of the Daytona Beach Bureau and a person I worked with and depended on for investigative support. Our working relationship had morphed into a personal friendship.

"Already talked to him about your opportunity. I asked him if I could approach you."

"Well, we're a long way from finding the money for a crime lab, and the city manager isn't on board with it. He'll be hard to convince."

"I've already been doing some research. Perhaps we could talk about it over dinner?" She winked at me.

I had learned right away that Torres was a flirt. How serious it was, I had no idea. And while the overtures had been flattering, there was no way I'd get involved with someone who worked for or with me.

I chuckled. "Everything is a little crazy right now. As soon as I have a break, I'll let you know and we can discuss it, but I make no promises."

"None required."

3

The diver showed up and loaded his gear alongside that of the crime scene team. The corporal backed the boat away from the slip and maneuvered into the Indian River. It was just after eight a.m., and I walked across the street to the PD, swiped my I.D. card through the reader at the employee entrance and weaved through the cubicles until I reached my office.

Martha Johnson was already at her desk.

"McCain. Can I have a word?"

I nodded, pulled keys from my pocket to open my office and unlocked the door.

She followed me in. "You haven't forgotten about talking to my boy?"

I walked around my desk, took a seat and observed Sergeant Martha Johnson. She was five feet tall and heavyset and wore her hair in a short masculine cut. Her light brown eyes were big, bright and cheerful. Her face was round, double-chinned and wrinkle-free.

"Nope. Today, right?"

"He hasn't been happy about it, but I told him to come here at two-thirty."

"Does he know what it's about?"

"He does. I told him, if he keeps hanging out with those boys, he is going to have trouble."

"And you think he'll listen to me?"

"I think if it's coming from *the man*, he might."

"We'll see," I said with little enthusiasm.

"I know this is a lot to ask. But he is a good boy, McCain.

15

"Tell me about him."

She stood in front of my desk, hands on her hips. Sarah James had warned me not to underestimate Johnson, that she, without fanfare, ran the department and commanded the respect of her peers and the command staff, who gave her wide latitude and hesitated to take her on.

I had looked over her personnel file after taking the chief position, and it shocked me to learn the extent of the woman's education and the educational accolades she'd accumulated. All uniformed officers in the PD were required to have at least a two-year degree in criminology from a police academy. She'd gone to Daytona State College's Police Academy and had earned her associates degree with a 4.0 average. She had become a Volusia County sheriff's deputy, then, a year later, had accepted a position with the Coronado PD.

It impressed me that after she'd signed on with Coronado, she'd continued her schooling. She'd gone on to the University of Central Florida and received a four-year degree in criminology, then a master's degree in business administration. She'd graduated from UCF with honors. All this she'd accomplished working full-time for the department and raising her son.

Martha Johnson stood almost at attention without answering me.

"Tell me about your son," I repeated.

What happened next was unexpected. Her shoulders softened like someone had let air out of her chest. Her eyes, which had been opened wide, narrowed. She blinked a few times, and I sensed she was holding back tears.

"May I sit, please?" she asked.

"Of course. Please." I gestured to a seat in front of my desk.

As she slumped into the chair, she exhaled. "I had Deshon when I was seventeen. I was the oldest of eleven children. My father was a drunk, and my mother, bless her heart, placed an incredible amount of responsibility on me. I had to quit school when I was in the ninth grade to take care of my siblings. I took up with an older man to get out of the house and soon became pregnant with Deshon. As soon as my man found out I was pregnant, he left me. If it weren't for Christian charity and a small Black church taking me in and helping me, I'd have been on the streets."

"You couldn't go home."

"Momma was drowning in her own troubles. There was no way I could add my burdens to hers. From there it has been an uphill battle. Raising a son as a single working mom has been difficult. This job pays poverty wages. If it weren't for the wonderful benefits and the fact that I'm a mile from my home, I'd have found work elsewhere.

"Deshon hasn't had it easy. Since he was in the ninth grade, he has been pretty much on his own. And smart? Through the eleventh grade, he was a straight A student. Never in any trouble, ever. He was on his way to a scholarship, but this year, Lord, he took up with some boys he calls his posse. Those boys have too much time on their hands and too little common sense.

"And I can't be the father he needs. He's missing a sense of family, the feeling of belonging to something larger than he is. He has no male role models, at least none exerting a positive influence, and he has been rejecting my leadership. I have no credibility with him, and now, because I'm a police officer, I've become the enemy. I'm hanging on to Deshon by a thread, McCain. I'm losing him, and this gang he has taken up with is exerting more influence."

"What's his response when you talk to him?"

"I get a lot of eye rolling, attitude and silence. When he does speak, I get one-word answers to my questions: 'nothing,' 'nowhere,' 'no one,' that sort of thing."

"Has he been in any legal trouble?"

"Nothing I haven't been able to fix. I owe many favors to folks in the department. Without them, he would have been charged or worse."

"What kinds of things has he done?"

"Petty theft. I've found things he couldn't have purchased in his room: cellphones, computers and video games. When I asked him where they came from, he said his friends gave them to him. When I ask where they obtained them, I get the 'I don't know,' a popular answer to most of my questions."

"What about this gang? What do you know about them?"

"You know anything about a city boy gang?"

"Sure. New York City was filled with them. Many are ethnic."

"Well, my boy and his posse, as he calls them, have a name, the Evil City Boys. The gang is out of Daytona, and the boys my son is involved with are part of it. I looked the name up on the internet. Everything I've learned from law enforcement says they're into moving stolen goods, extortion for protection and moving drugs. Until now, I've kept Deshon out of serious trouble. Unfortunately, the pull of this gang is strong, and the things they're involved in are escalating. With each escalation, I'm having more difficulty getting through to him."

"What's he good at?"

"Two very inconsistent things. He's a math whiz. He soars off the charts in aptitude for math and science."

"The inconsistency?"

"He's a gifted artist, McCain." Tears started to flow down her cheeks. "You should see his oil paintings. That boy has such a talent." She was quiet for a moment, trying to regain her composure. "I'm losing him."

"Let me talk to him. I don't know what I can do, but I'm willing to try."

"That's all I can ask."

Martha Johnson stood up, "This discussion is between you and me, right?"

"Your secret's safe with me."

"It best be, McCain."

There was the faintest grin on her lips as she turned and headed out of my office.

My cellphone rang. It was Downs.

"We have nothing."

"Did the diver find anything?"

"A beer can and some bottle caps. From the looks of them, they've been in the water a long time."

"Did Torres find anything?"

"McCain, there's nothing."

"Call the county and surrounding PDs and alert them to any Missing Person reports. Tell them we're looking for a young woman."

"I already have one of my people working on it. I'll let you know when we have something."

"Downs, when you smelled the woman's breath, was there an odor of almonds?"

"You know, I thought I caught a whiff of it, but if I did, it was faint. Nothing I could swear to. Are you thinking poison?"

"Yes. Call Hunter about it, will you?"

"Already did. He said he would check into it, but he didn't sound too optimistic. He's going to check to see if there's increased adrenalin in the blood. You've worked cyanide cases before. Traces of the poison vanish quickly, and it has been eight hours since TOD."

"It could be nothing; it could be everything. Did Hunter say when he would finish the autopsy?"

"He's working it now. I'm going to run by the morgue and catch the tail end of the autopsy. I'll call you when he's done."

4

I put the phone down in the cradle, and Johnson appeared at the door. "Jarret wants you in his office. He didn't say please."

I walked across to the City Hall employee entrance. Jarret's office was large enough to accommodate a desk and credenza, two guest chairs and a conference table with four chairs. I had learned most routine meetings and discussions took place at the conference table, but when he wanted to lord it over me, he sat behind his desk with me in a guest chair. When I knocked on the doorframe, he remained behind his desk.

"Is this about the crime lab?" I asked.

"You know damn well it is." Jarret was nearly bald with a ribbon of dark blond hair that looked like a crown. Although he was heavyset, he carried it well. He wore a white long-sleeved shirt and a red and white striped tie. "We've talked about this, McCain. Several times."

I liked Neil Jarret. He was professional, a talented administrator and a good teacher. When I took this job, while I'd had supervisory experience with the NYPD, I had known nothing about budgeting or administration, and even less about all the personnel issues a chief must deal with. Jarret, when he'd hired me, had committed to teaching me. I had learned a lot from him and had much more to learn. I held him in high regard.

"Do you want to hear my side of this?" I asked.

"All right." He sat back in his high-backed chair, adjusted his black-rimmed glasses and straightened his tie.

"AJ asked me, soon after Sarah's death, why the FDLE was involved in investigating a death in Coronado Beach. I was sitting on my dock having a beer, and he walked over, sat down beside me and started asking questions. This was just before the council appointed him to fill David Parker's mayoral seat. I explained to him the FDLE services the city uses. He asked me if it'd be better if we had our own crime lab. I gave him my opinion. That's it. That's all the discussion I had with him. I had no idea at the time he would end up mayor."

"So, you're telling me you had no idea he would bring up the crime lab at the city council meeting?"

"No. That was the only time I discussed it with him."

"You didn't think to tell me about your discussion with him?"

"There wasn't a discussion. He asked me a question, and I answered him. I had no idea he was anything more than curious. I had no idea he would take it up as a cause. He had given me no indication of that."

"You should have told me about it, McCain. The city doesn't have the money to establish its own lab. Now we're all going to spend a lot of time and money proving to the council we can't afford to do this without raising taxes, something I've no intention of doing." He leaned forward in his seat. "Your relationship with the mayor must come to an end. I told you when I hired you that having a relationship with the mayor or council members was out of bounds. I warned you I'd not tolerate you having communications with them around this office."

"You make it sound like I haven't honored our agreement. I told you I'd follow chain of command, and I have."

"If you had followed chain of command, none of this would have happened."

"We need to go over a few things, Mr. Jarret. First, when I bought my house, I had no idea AJ McFarland lived next door. I had no idea he was on the city council and didn't know about it until after you and the council considered firing me over the Night Fire killings. I've never made any overtures to develop a relationship with AJ. He imposed himself on me. He had just lost his wife; he was lonely and sought me out. When I lost Sarah, he was someone to lean on, and AJ convinced me to stay on as chief.

"I've never discussed police business with him unless asked. I have not and I will not discuss a case with him. I can count three or four times he has asked me about things with the department that were trivial. Since he was elected mayor, he has never asked me anything about the department. All our discussions are personal."

"That's unacceptable, McCain."

"What isn't acceptable?"

"Your personal relationship with the mayor undermines my authority and interferes with decisions I have to make with regard to the police department. It is obvious that if you and I have a disagreement, he'll take your side."

"Has that happened yet?"

"No, but I discussed his proposed crime lab study and shared with him my concern that it is a luxury we can't afford, and he blew me off. He has his mind made up on the matter."

"I can't help that. I've done nothing to provoke this."

"Nothing? Then how did he come up with the idea?"

"He asked me a question. At the time, I had no idea he was involved with the city."

"This isn't going to work, McCain."

"What do you expect me to do?"

"End your relationship with the mayor."

"And how do you propose I do that? He lives next door to me."

"That isn't my problem. We had an agreement. I suffered for five years with your predecessor's politicking, and I've no intention of spending the next five years living through that with you."

I stood up. It was all I could do to control my anger.

"I gave you my word I'd follow chain of command. I give you my word now that I'll not initiate discussion with McFarland on anything related to this department, but he's the mayor. If he asks me a question, I'll answer it. And I'll not end my friendship with him. Since he has been mayor, there hasn't been one time we've discussed department business. The way I look at it, he's your boss. If you don't want him talking to me or asking me questions about the department, you should take that up with him."

Jarret was silent. It was apparent the discussion hadn't gone in the direction he'd hoped. Neither of us budged.

"Mr. Jarret—Neil—I don't need a problem. My badge is yours to take. If that's what you want, I'll clear out, and you can find another chief. AJ has been a real friend to me when I needed it, and I'll not do anything to harm him."

Jarret sat there, his silence and stoic look screaming his disapproval.

"Well, until you tell me different, I've a department to run and a murder to solve." I turned and headed for the door.

"Murder?"

I stopped and turned around in the doorway. "We found a girl on Disappearing Island this morning. When I have more, I'll fill you in."

"McCain? This isn't personal. I like you, but I'm not going to repeat the political bullshit I went through with Chief Grizzle, with you or anyone else. Consider this your two-week notice."

"I must tell you, I'm disappointed. I thought we worked well together. When you hired me, you said if things didn't work out as chief, I could go back to being a homicide detective. Is that still possible?"

"I'm sorry, McCain. That wouldn't work for me, I'm afraid. I'll be sending a letter to the mayor and city council within the hour advising them of my decision. In the meantime, I'm asking you not to discuss this with anyone until the council is aware of my decision and I make the announcement public. I'd appreciate your cooperation on that."

Jarret began to shuffle papers on his desk, my cue to leave.

When I arrived back at my office, Jim Cahill was there, pacing back and forth. I walked in, closed and locked the door, and slumped into one of the guest chairs in front of my desk.

"You look like you've been mugged, McCain."

"You could say that."

"Well, are you going to tell me what's going on, or do I have to use enhanced interrogation techniques?"

Cahill was five-ten with a shock of jet-black hair he parted in the center and a full black mustache. His suits were expensive, his mannerisms disarming, and, after Sarah's death, as I had been digging myself out of grief, we'd occupied barstools together on many an occasion.

"Jarret just fired me."

"What! Say that again." Cahill dropped into the other chair next to me. He leaned forward, placing his elbows on his knees, and looked straight at me.

"Jarret just fired me. He gave me my two-week notice. You need to keep this on the down-low until he informs the council."

"For what?"

"Because of my friendship with the mayor."

"You're serious."

"The last chief, Grizzle, lobbied the former mayor and council members to the point Jarret lost control over the police department. Although Grizzle reported to Jarret, Grizzle had the political juice with the council to ignore Jarret, and Jarret was afraid to take him on. When Grizzle resigned and Jarret offered me the job, he made a point of telling me he wouldn't tolerate that kind of arrangement in the future; I had to direct my communication about the department to him alone. And I agreed to that."

"So, what's the problem?"

"AJ McFarland is my neighbor."

"The mayor?"

"The same. When I bought my house, I had no idea he lived next door. We've become friends. Now, Jarret feels threatened."

"I saw an article in the *News Journal* about Coronado Beach's desire to build a crime lab. Does that have anything to do with this?"

"Everything. Sorry I didn't tell you about that. I had no idea AJ was going to bring it before the council. I was as surprised as everyone else."

"What're you going to do, Jed?"

"Jarret wants me to sell my house, move somewhere else and tell AJ I'm cutting off all contact with him. I can't do that. He has been a good friend to me."

"Well, I have an opening for a special agent. It will take several weeks to go through the vetting process..."

"I appreciate the offer, Jim. I feel like this is the beginning of the process, not the end."

"Welcome to the world of small-town politics. Sometimes it's the Wild West."

"What do you mean?"

"City-elected officials are lay people. They come from all occupations. Most haven't the first clue about what it takes to run an organization the size of Coronado Beach. While some have altruistic motives, many council members run for office for the perks and the prestige that goes with the office. Once elected, their main goal is to stay in office. To do that, they take up causes to prove to the electorate that they've accomplished something. So, they meddle in the operations of the city. In my experience, the police department is the easiest target for controversy. I can understand why Jarret is sensitive about chain of command.

"Another tempting area for council persons to meddle in is city employee issues, like pay or benefits, or grievances employees have with the way they're treated."

I asked, "What would the council gain by getting involved with employee issues?"

"Votes. The city has about three hundred employees, many of whom are registered voters. Very often the difference between a councilperson winning office or not depends on who the city employees support. It doesn't take long for those running for office, or trying to keep their seats on the council, to learn they need city employees to do so. It gives employees a lot of power. They can demand pay and other benefits in exchange for their support."

"That's a conflict of interest, isn't it?"

"Sure, it is. Nonetheless, it's a reality managers in government need to understand and come to terms with. That includes chiefs of police. Jarret was burned badly in the past by the previous chief."

"So, are you telling me you think he's right?"

"No, but I understand where he's coming from. There are small cities we provide services to where council members, chiefs of police and mayors conduct open warfare against each other. Where city government is toxic, gridlock results. Jarret has done a good job keeping that kind of chaos out of Coronado Beach. Grizzle was the exception and a thorn in Jarret's side."

"I think what he's asking is unreasonable. I understand he wants to control things, but dictating whom I befriend is over the line. When the mayor or council members ask me a question about the operation of the department, what am I supposed to do, refuse to answer their question?"

"No, but you could refer them to the city manager. You could just say it would be more appropriate for them to direct their question through the manager. That would be the proper procedure."

"Assuming you're right, how would you deal with the mayor being my next-door neighbor?"

"I guess it all boils down to how much do you want to keep this job?"

"It seems to me there has to be some trust here. I don't think I want to be in a position where I'm looking over my shoulder or stressing out over what I say to people. Jarret asked me to direct police business through him, and I've done that. If he doesn't trust me, then I shouldn't be in the job."

"I think that's the heart of the issue."

Silence filled the space for a few moments.

Cahill said, "Jarret and I have a good relationship. Do you want me to talk to him?"

"No, I'd prefer you didn't. I need to think about this."

"Maybe I could buy you a little more time. Once Jarret makes his announcement, it may be too late to undo this."

"No, Jim. I'm not prepared to meet his demands. I don't want this job if I have to agree to something rigid."

"If you change your mind..."

"I know, and I appreciate your willingness to help."

"Tell me about the body you found this morning."

"Torres must have called you. There is nothing much to tell. We have a young Jane Doe. Except for inconclusive signs someone may have poisoned her, we've no evidence on the body or at the scene that gives us a clue to how she died. I stress the 'may' part because we have suspicions and no hard evidence.

"Torres will run the pictures of the woman through facial recognition and see if we can find something, perhaps a driver's license."

"Downs went to the morgue to follow up on the autopsy. We should hear something on that this morning."

Cahill stood and made his way to the door. "If I can help with Jarret, let me know."

"Thanks."

He unlocked the door, opened it and left.

I decided against calling AJ. He would hear soon enough. This was the part of the chief's job I hated: the politics.

Within the hour, I received a call from Downs.

"County 911 called me a moment ago. They have a Missing Person report of a young woman matching our victim. A Chad Belford reported his girlfriend, Victoria Rockwell, missing at nine-thirty this morning."

"You have an address?"

"I'm on my way to the PD to get you. I called Belford, and we're going to meet with him at their condo."

"Anything from the autopsy?"

"I'll tell you when I get there."

5

I was anxious to get out of the PD and clear my head. As I thought through all my options with Jarret, none of them offered a satisfactory solution. I walked out of the employee entrance and waited for Downs in the parking lot.

Downs stopped her silver Dodge Charger, I climbed in, and Downs reversed course through town, up over the South Causeway Bridge and over to beachside.

"Anything from the autopsy?"

"Just a list of all the things we haven't found."

"Any signs of cyanide?"

"Not exactly. Hunter did find elevated adrenalin levels in her blood. Before he opened her up, he tested her blood for cyanide but didn't find anything. He was quick to point out that it didn't mean someone hadn't poisoned her. The fact that we both observed a pinkish hue to her skin and a faint almond smell on her breath points to poisoning as a potential cause of death. He warned that without something more definitive, poisoning would be difficult to prove. He won't list it as a cause of death unless he can prove it. He said the raised adrenalin levels could have resulted from a fight or flight response to a life-or-death situation."

"There were no indications of violence?"

"None. You know Hunter. He won't rule in anything without the proof to support it."

"What about tissue samples? There may be residue of cyanide in the tissue."

"He's sending samples to FDLE's crime lab for analysis."

"Anything else?"

"The woman was pregnant."

"Pregnant?"

"Yep. About two months along, and she had breast implants."

"Any serial numbers that would help identify her?"

"Hunter's working on it."

"Anything on her clothes? Tox screen?"

"It will be a day or two before we have that."

"So, we have nothing."

"For now."

Downs turned south along the ocean on A1A toward Bethune Beach. Near Bethune, the Manchester, an eight-story luxury oceanfront condo, towered over single-family homes wedged up against the dunes on the ocean's edge. Downs pulled up to a security gate, badged the guard and found a guest parking space in the underground garage.

We found the elevator, and Downs pushed the button labeled "penthouse." The elevator deposited us in a foyer on the eighth floor. Two condos took up the entire floor. Downs pushed the doorbell for 8B. A moment later, a young man in his mid-twenties with shoulder-length sun-bleached blond hair answered the door. He was dressed in a white Rip Curl T-shirt and flowered knee-length baggies. His face was long and thin, and he had brown eyes and sported a two-day growth of beard.

"You must be the police."

"Lieutenant Downs, and this is Chief McCain. We're with the Coronado Beach Police Department." She showed him her badge and re-clipped it to her belt. "Are you Chad Belford?"

"Did you find Vicky?"

"May we come in, please?"

Belford opened the door wide. "Come in."

We walked through a short hall with a half-bath to the right and into an expansive space that doubled as a living and dining area. To the front was a solid glass wall with a view of the ocean. Along the back wall was a large kitchen with an impressive island that separated the kitchen from the living space. To the left, a hallway led to what I presumed to be bedrooms, and to the right was a doorway to a master suite. The condo was a corner unit with glass that curved around the front to the side. As I moved into the space, I could see a wide balcony to the right with three chaise lounges, a small bar and a sliding glass door to access it. The floors were white marble. The furnishings were modern with white leather. Splashes of bright color in the lamps and sculptures gave the room a festive appearance.

Belford escorted us to the glass-topped dining table with wheeled leather chairs. He flipped his hair out of his face and eased into one of the chairs, and we sat down with him.

Downs said, "We're following up on your call to 911 about a young woman who may be missing."

"Vicky. We live together. She didn't make it home last night, and she wasn't home this morning when I woke up. So, I called 911."

"Do you have a picture of her? One we could take with us."

"Yeah. Just a minute." He stood up from the table, walked through the door to the master bedroom and returned with a four by six photograph. He handed the photo to Downs; she looked at it and handed it to me.

There was no doubt the woman in the picture was the woman we'd found that morning.

Downs looked at me, and I knew she was hesitant, undecided on which of us would tell Belford about his girlfriend.

I said, "I'm sorry to report we found your Victoria Rockwell's body on Disappearing Island this morning."

Belford swept his hair off his face. "She's dead?"

"Yes. We're sorry. When did you see her last?"

"You can't be serious! How did she die?"

"We don't know yet," Downs said. "We just found her a couple of hours ago."

"Where did you say you found her?"

I remained silent and let Downs handle the interview.

She said, "Disappearing Island. It is a large sandbar in the Intracoastal Waterway near Ponce Inlet. It is only accessible by boat."

"How did she get there?"

"We were hoping you might be able to tell us."

"I have no idea. You say she's dead?" Tears welled in Belford's eyes. He inhaled deeply, wiped his eyes and tried to retain control.

"When did you see her last, Mr. Belford?"

"Yesterday afternoon, about three. I went surfing, and when I arrived home, she was gone."

"Do you know where she went?"

"No."

"Where did you go surfing?"

"Canaveral National Seashore."

"What time did you get back to the condo?"

"Around seven. Vicky left me a note. She said she would be out for the evening."

"Do you still have the note she left you?"

"I tossed it in the trash can under the sink in the kitchen. Do you want me to get it?"

"Yes, please."

Belford pushed his chair away from the table, padded into the kitchen, rattled around under the sink, returned with a slip of pink paper and handed it to Downs. She looked it over and handed it to me. It was Post-it paper with a sticky backing. The handwriting was neat and flowing. *C, out for the evening. I'll wake you when I get in. Pizza in the frig. V.*

"You're her boyfriend, and you have no idea where she could have gone?" Downs asked.

"Vicky has many friends and is very active. She could have been doing anything."

"You don't think it is a little odd she wouldn't let you know where she was going?"

"We just don't have that kind of relationship."

"Then how would you describe your relationship?"

"Casual. I live with her, but not all the time."

I asked, "What kind of work do you do, Chad?"

"Laminator. I work on surfboards and paddleboards."

Downs followed up with, "Who do you work for?"

"I work as a sub-contractor. There are several surfboard and paddleboard manufacturers between here and West Palm Beach, and I do work for all of them."

"Where do you live when you don't live here?"

"I have an RV. When I'm down south working, I live in it."

I looked around at this penthouse condo, and it was obvious Chad Belford wasn't making the kind of money to afford the place.

Downs continued, "What kind of work did Ms. Rockwell do?"

"She did different things. She modeled some. She did event planning. She was into lots of things."

"What kind of events?" Downs was scribbling on her notepad as she asked questions.

"Social parties, political events and special events."

"Social parties?"

"People hire her to host parties at their homes. She would organize them, arrange for entertainment, send invitations, rent equipment, provide transportation and manage the event."

"She would have to be doing pretty well to be able to afford a place like this."

"I wouldn't know."

I asked, "You described your relationship as casual. What do you mean?"

"As far as Vicky was concerned, we were friends with benefits."

"You mean sexual benefits."

"Yes. Vicky didn't like living here alone. She didn't feel safe. So, I stayed with her."

"You used the phrase 'as far as Vicky was concerned.' How would you describe your relationship with her?" Downs asked.

"I'm in love with her...or I should say I *was* in love with her."

"Were you aware your companion was pregnant?"

"Pregnant?" Chad flipped his long hair over his shoulder, and he struggled again to keep his composure. "This is the first I've heard about that."

I asked, "Where were you between ten and midnight last night?"

"You think I had something to do with Vicky's death?"

"Our investigation is just beginning, Mr. Belford. We're just collecting information."

"I watched TV until around ten-thirty, went to bed and woke up about six this morning."

"And you weren't concerned when your companion didn't show up before you went to bed?" I asked.

"No. She's gone in the evenings and doesn't get home until well after midnight. She's always home, though, before I wake up in the morning."

"So, if she's always out late, what prompted you to call 911 this morning?" Downs asked.

"I just didn't have a good feeling when I woke up this morning."

"And what made you feel that way?"

"You would have to know Vicky. Vicky is fearless—in-your-face fearless. She never sees the danger in anything. When she was out in the evening without me, I always worried she would get herself into a situation she couldn't handle. This morning, when she didn't show up, I just had a bad feeling about it."

Downs said, "A moment ago, you made it sound like you stayed here because she was afraid to be alone. And now you're saying she was fearless."

"She wasn't physically afraid to be alone. She just didn't handle being alone very well."

"You mean emotionally?"

"Maybe, I don't know. All I know is she didn't want to be alone."

"You said you stayed in your RV on occasion when you worked down south."

"She didn't care for that. She made it plain to me."

"But..."

"There's no but. We were compatible. Sexually and otherwise. She didn't like it when I was gone, and she let me know how she felt."

"She was not in love with you, though."

"No."

"Why not? You said you were compatible."

"The most important thing in Vicky's life was Vicky. There wasn't enough room in Vicky to love someone else."

"And you still loved her?"

"Yes. I'm a sick shit, I know."

"Were you the only one she was sexually involved with?"

"She told me once she could never be faithful to just one man. We never talked about it after that."

"You didn't answer my question."

"No. I'm not the only one."

"What makes you say that?"

"I just know. Look, I know you're just doing your job, but I didn't have anything to do with what happened to Vicky, whatever happened to her. I loved her. So, are we done here?"

I looked at Downs, and she nodded to me. "I just have a few more questions."

"Okay," Belford said, cutting a sideways glance at me.

"Did Vicky have family or close friends?"

"I asked her once about her family, and she refused to discuss them with me. Friends? I've been with Vicky for just over a year. If she had friends, I'm not aware of any."

"Do you know of any reason someone might want to harm Vicky? Did she have any enemies?"

"Vicky was all about the businesses she was in. Vicky's closest friend was herself. If she had enemies, I wouldn't know them."

"Did you ever accompany her to any of the events or parties she hosted?"

"No. I never did. Like I said, that was separate."

Downs stood, and Belford and I stood at the same time.

"What'll happen to her place and her belongings?" He looked around the palatial space.

Downs said, "I don't know. If she had no will, or didn't leave instructions, we would try to find next of kin, and they'll make those decisions. Do you think she would have had a will?"

"I doubt it. Do I need to leave here?"

"I wish I could advise you," I said. "Did Vicky own the condo?"

"You know, I have no idea whether she owned it or rented it."

"We may have more questions later."

"You think someone killed Vicky, don't you?"

"We just don't know yet. Thank you for talking with us," I said. "We'll show ourselves out."

"One other thing," Downs said. "When you saw her last, what was she wearing?"

"Tan shorts and a white sleeveless blouse."

Downs asked, "What's your cellphone number?"

He gave it to her.

"Thank you, Mr. Belford." She handed him a card and asked him to call us if he thought of anything that might be helpful to us.

When we walked down to the car, Downs wrote her recollections on her notepad. I started to ask for her impression of Belford, but she shushed me, held up a finger and continued to write. It took her several minutes to finish her notes.

"You want to know what I think." It was a statement, not a question. "That was strange. It sounded to me like

Belford was nothing more than a sex toy and sleepover companion."

"Do you think he could be the father of her child?" I asked.

"Beats me. A simple DNA test would tell us. I think we ought to get a search warrant for the condo and an order for a paternity test for Belford."

"Yeah, the circumstances are suspicious. Let's find out if a judge will go for it."

"I'll work on it when we get back to the PD. What's your take?"

"I have all kinds of questions. I find it odd that she was secretive with him about her work, like she had something to hide. It bothers me that the kid knows nothing about her family and friends and has been living with her for over a year. I find it odd the woman is pregnant, and the man she has been having regular sex with believes there are other men who also could be the father. The condo is a two to three million-dollar unit. I don't know what an event planner makes, but it takes some serious jack to pay for a place like that. While you're getting a warrant, make sure it covers all of her financial and phone records as well."

When we made it back to the PD, Johnson came into the office and slid a piece of paper onto the blotter on my desk.

"Cahill faxed this over. It's about that woman y'all found this morning."

I sat down at the desk and examined the picture. It was a blown-up driver license photo. It matched the woman we'd pulled from the Indian River that morning. Her name was not Victoria, and the last name was not Rockwell. The name on the DL was Sally Patricia McCoy.

Given her date of birth, she was twenty-six years old, five-foot-five and one hundred ten pounds. Her hair was brown, but there was no mistaking her high cheekbones and blue eyes. The DL was issued seven years ago. The address given on the license was on the mainland side of town.

I walked out to Johnson's cubicle. "Run her name through the system and see what we get. I doubt this woman, McCoy, still lives at this address, but check anyway. See who owns it."

"Okay, I'll take care of it."

It was almost eleven, and I was sure that as deliberate and organized as Neil Jarret was, the announcement of my dismissal should have hit the fan by now. It would be lunchtime before word spread through the department, and when it did, Leslie Downs blew into my office.

"What I'm hearing *cannot* be true."

I said, "It would help if you could give me a clue what you're talking about."

"I heard you were fired."

"The rumor is true."

She eased into the chair in front of my desk and curled her red hair around her ears. "What the hell did you do?"

"Nothing. It seems the mayor is my neighbor and my friend. That's a huge conflict of interest for me. One the city manager feels he can't live with."

"AJ McFarland is your neighbor? I had no idea. Well, I knew your house was in the same subdivision as his, but I never gave the relationship a thought."

"Mr. Jarret has given it plenty of thought."

41

"I can't believe he's doing this to you. I had just started to enjoy my job again."

"Don't be too hard on him, Downs. One of the conditions I agreed to when I took the job was, I'd not have communications with the city council outside the chain of command. Chief Grizzle was notorious for that, and it made Jarret's job very difficult. I had no idea when I bought my house that AJ, I mean Mayor McFarland, was my next-door neighbor. Of course, he wasn't mayor then, he was on the council. I didn't mean to violate our agreement, but I guess I have. When Sarah James was killed, that was a rough patch for me. AJ was there and helped me through it."

"Anything I can do?"

"Yep, you can help me find out who killed Sally McCoy."

"Who's that?"

"That's the real name of the woman we found this morning. At some point, she changed her name. I have Johnson checking her for prior arrests."

"Chief?" It was Johnson at the door to my office with a small knot of people behind her.

"Come in."

Behind Johnson were Commanders John Hocking, community affairs, and Tom Morris, operations.

I said, "Y'all must have heard."

They all nodded in unison.

I spent a few moments summarizing my dismissal. I emphasized what I had just told Downs. "This is an unfortunate situation that just happened. Jarret had every right to do what he did. I understand why and can find no fault in his reasoning. He's a good man."

Hocking, a tall man with black hair graying at the temples, asked, "Is there any way to fix this?"

"Yes, but I'm unwilling to do what he asked me to do."

Morris, in his early thirties, heavyset, with a blond crew cut asked, "So, who's going to take your place?"

"I'll be chief for the next two weeks, and I'm willing to stay until they find my replacement. Until then, nothing changes. Right now, we have a city to protect, a murder to solve and jobs to do. So, let's get to it."

They all left except for Martha Johnson and Downs.

Johnson pulled a slip of paper from her dark blue uniform pants pocket.

"On Sally McCoy, the address on her driver license belongs to Patrick and Verna McCoy. Sally McCoy has several hits: one for petty larceny, which never made it to court; one for prostitution, which they knocked down to a misdemeanor, a fine and time served; and a misdemeanor for possession of marijuana. She also has a sealed juvie record. No felonies."

"Sounds like the McCoys are family," Downs said.

I said to both of them, "Let's go get something to eat. Afterwards, we'll go talk to the McCoys."

Johnson said, "Y'all go without me. I have to see about my boy. You haven't forgotten about this afternoon, Chief?"

"I'll be here in time."

"Since Johnson isn't going with us, let's talk to the McCoys first, McCain. If we eat first, my mind will be mush."

The McCoy home was five blocks from the PD, south of town in an older neighborhood. The house was a small single-story block home that appeared to be 1950-ish architecture. The large yard was crowded with several sixty-plus-year-old live oak trees adorned with low-hanging Spanish moss.

When we approached the front door, several wasps floated around a hive that hung underneath the porch light. Once we pushed the doorbell, we stood away from the door to avoid getting stung.

A woman in her late forties, of medium height and weight with a round face, disheveled short brown hair and thin lips, answered the door on the second ring.

"Mrs. McCoy?"

She stood behind a screened aluminum-framed door. "Yes. What's this about?"

"I'm Chief McCain, and this is Lieutenant Leslie Downs. We're with the Coronado Beach Police Department. Are you related to Sally McCoy?"

"What has she done now?"

"Are you her mother?"

"Yes, biologically."

"May we come in for a moment?"

"What's this about?" she asked again. She wore a loose-fitting yellow T-shirt, and cheater reading glasses hung from her neck on a chain.

"It would be better if we discussed this inside."

I could see her pupils enlarge, and her face flushed. Without responding, she pushed the screen door open and led us into a small living area. The floral print couch and matching wingback chairs were dated. The house was dark, with sheer white curtains covering the picture window between the living room and the front porch. All the tables in the room were caked with dust, and the smell of mold and stale air filled the room.

Downs and I both sat on the couch, perched on the edge of the cushions. Mrs. McCoy sat in the chair closest to us.

McCoy said, "Why is it you've come to see me?"

"We're sorry to report, we found your daughter's body on Disappearing Island this morning in the Intracoastal Waterway."

"She's dead?"

"We're sorry, Mrs. McCoy," Downs offered. "We know how you must feel."

The woman sat in silence without expression for a few moments, then said, "You have no idea how I feel. Don't you presume you do."

Silence.

Downs looked at me, and I let the silence drag out, waiting for McCoy to say something.

After an uncomfortable few minutes, she said, "I wish I could say I was sorry my daughter was dead. It doesn't surprise me."

I looked at Downs to gauge her reaction to what the woman had just said.

McCoy continued, "She was a beautiful girl, but on the inside, she was the devil incarnate." The woman looked at me and moved forward in her seat. "That girl was pure evil."

"Why do you say that, Mrs. McCoy?"

"Are you familiar with the term sociopath?"

"Yes," I said.

"Our daughter was a sociopath in the extreme."

"How do you think this bears on her death?"

"How did she die?"

"We aren't sure yet. We're in the beginning of our investigation."

"Do you suspect someone killed her?"

"Why? Do you think someone killed her?" I asked.

"You would have to understand my daughter and her history to understand there's a long line of people who'd cheer if they knew she was dead."

"Perhaps you could explain."

"There's nothing Sally wouldn't do to get what she wanted: lie, steal and extort. She would slander anyone and destroy anyone. Right and wrong meant nothing to her."

"Could you give us an example?" I asked.

"You know how you'd receive preapproved credit card solicitations before they banned the practice? When Sally was fourteen, she would open these solicitations, fill them out and return them without our knowledge. At the time, I had a full-time job, and neither my husband nor I would be home to get the mail. These credit cards would arrive, and Sally would take cash advances and make large purchases. Before we realized what was going on, she'd run up twenty-five thousand dollars in debt. It nearly ruined us.

"Then, three years later, she wanted this car, a convertible, a Mustang convertible. We couldn't afford it. We were still struggling from the credit cards she ran up. We refused to give her the money. We received a call from our bank that Sally had tried to get access to ten thousand dollars in CDs we'd set aside for our retirement. She forged our signature on withdrawal documents and told the bank branch manager we'd given her a birthday present to buy a car. Good for us, the manager knew the past issues we had had with our daughter and called us. She was eighteen then, and that's when we threw her out."

I said, "She has a sealed juvenile record. Did you ever bring charges against her for the credit card theft and attempted theft at the bank?"

"No, we didn't press charges, but she conned one of her girlfriends in school into doing the same thing. The girls went on a spending spree. The other girl's parents pressed charges against Sally. Since their own daughter had taken part in the theft and there was no way to charge Sally without also charging their daughter, they dropped charges, and the police never pressed it.

"Sally skipped school all the time. The police were involved. Once they determined we'd done everything within our power to make sure she went to school, she went to juvenile court for truancy and spent a week in detention. She was sixteen when they released her, but she still refused to go to school. The principal expelled her. We tried to get her a job, but she refused to work. She would leave for days at a time, and it happened so often, we stopped calling the police. Just before her seventeenth birthday, the police arrested her for possession. We refused to bail her out. She talked one of her old boyfriends into posting her bail after several days in jail and managed to get off with a light sentence. It was after that she tried to steal money from our CDs."

"When was the last time you had contact with your daughter?"

"Two years after we asked her to leave, she came by the house wanting money. She must have been twenty then. She gave us some phony story about being pregnant and needing money to go to the doctor. We were convinced she wanted the money for drugs, and we refused. Then we heard she had a boob job. By then, our relationship with Sally had been destroyed."

Reading from her notes, Downs said, "You indicated there were several people who'd be happy to learn she was dead."

"Sally used people, Detective. I can only imagine, the way she treated us, her own flesh and blood, how she would treat others."

"So, you can't name those who might have wanted to harm her?"

"No, but I know my daughter. I know how evil she was. I just don't think you'll have to look hard to find someone who'd have wanted her dead."

"Did you want her dead, Mrs. McCoy?" I asked.

"Wanting to and doing something about it are two different things. She made our lives hell, Chief McCain. One of the happiest days of my life was when she left our home. You have no idea what that girl was capable of. No idea."

"We would like to interview Mr. McCoy. Where does he work?"

"Patrick is a cement truck driver for a local concrete and materials company. You can catch him before he leaves for the plant in the morning, or when he gets home around six-thirty in the evening. Why would you want to talk to him? He's going to tell you the same thing I told you."

"Just procedure," I said. "We want to talk to all the people in her life. The more we know, the better equipped we are to find those who might have wanted to harm your daughter." I handed her my card. "If you can think of anything that might help us, give us a call."

McCoy nodded.

When I walked out the door, I wondered what else we would find out about Sally McCoy.

6

Downs and I drove across town to Outriggers and sat at an outside table overlooking the marina, and both of us ordered fish and drinks. The humidity was high, and a strong offshore breeze blew through the patio. The yachts berthed in the marina rocked against their moorings.

When my beer arrived, Downs said, "I've never seen you order a beer when you're on duty."

"What're they going to do, fire me?"

"You have a point."

"The girl with the angelic face we found this morning isn't sounding angelic."

"It's pretty bad when you can't even count on your own mother to vouch for you."

"In New York, I investigated every possible motive for murder. I wish I could say that what Mrs. McCoy reported about her daughter was unusual. Drug addicts are capable of anything."

"McCain, she was talking about issues with her daughter that pre-dated drugs. Do you think it is possible kids can come from the womb predisposed to criminality?"

"Do you mean some sort of genetic flaw?"

"Yes. Do you believe that? Like our victim. Her mother says she was a sociopath like it was part of her from birth." Downs' voice was expressive, her elbows were on the table, and she leaned her body forward into our conversation.

"The experts say not. They say criminal behavior has more to do with environmental influences than genetics.

That doesn't explain how the same parents can raise two children—good parents—and one child becomes a serial killer, while the other is normal in every respect. I've seen many cases where children with horrible parents walk in horror as adults."

"Is that what you think happened with our victim?"

"Mrs. McCoy seemed normal enough, though she could have been a monster to her child for all we know. Until we dig deeper, we have no idea. I'm not willing to accept her mother's explanation at face value. We need to understand the victim's proclivities before we begin to draw conclusions."

Downs pushed back into her seat and dropped her hands into her lap. "So, what are you going to do?"

"You mean jobwise?"

She nodded.

"I don't know. Cahill said he could use an experienced investigator in his office. The nice thing about my situation is my NYPD retirement provides a decent income. I don't have to do anything."

"I can't imagine you sitting still for five minutes much less for the rest of your life. You're too young to retire."

"You're right, but I've thoughts of buying a boat and learning how to fish."

"Ah huh. You've been here a little more than six months. Have you even tried to fish?"

"No."

"Have you even looked at a boat with the thought of buying one?"

"I haven't had the chance, Downs."

"If it was something you wanted to do, you would have done it by now."

"All of a sudden you're a career counselor?"

"Jed, you love the work too much." It was the first time Downs had called me by my first name.

"There's that."

"And you've done a good job."

"I appreciate you saying that Downs."

"You should fight it. The people in the department will support you."

"I appreciate what you're trying to do, but I don't want to wage a war. If I fought Jarret and I won, he could make life miserable for me. I don't want that."

"I have no idea what you would have to do to keep the job, but I hope you can find a solution and stay."

"Thanks. I appreciate your kind words."

The server brought our fish, and conversation was light until we finished our meal.

I looked at my watch and panicked. "I have to get back to the PD." I signaled our server for a check.

Downs said, "Can I ask you something personal?"

"Shoot."

"Why haven't you ever asked me to go out with you?"

The question took me aback. "Wow, that is personal."

I watched Leslie Downs. She was attractive, and under different circumstances, very attractive. I had to admit, in the last month, as the grief I'd experienced at Sarah's death had softened, I had found my interactions with Downs more comfortable and comforting.

She said, "That was over the line. I'm sorry."

"No, no. It's a fair question. If things were different, I would have, but we work together. The department has an anti-frat policy for good reasons. If we were involved and the relationship went south, it would be hell having to work together."

"Well, if you're not with the department any longer..."

"That's a bridge we haven't crossed yet."

"Just curious, Jed, that's all. If you'd asked me, the answer would have been yes."

"We need to go. I have someone waiting for me in my office."

"You need to fight to keep your job, McCain."

When I arrived at my office, Deshon Johnson was pacing back and forth in front of my desk.

When I stepped into the office, he stood still and faced me without expression. Unlike Martha Johnson, he was tall, six-foot-four perhaps, and at least two hundred pounds. His skin was much darker than his mother's. He wore a white strap T-shirt and new baggy denim pants. The legs were too long and bunched up at his untied white designer basketball shoes. On his left shoulder was a single tattoo, an Oriental symbol or lettering I didn't recognize. The skin around it looked red, as though the tattoo might be new. His beard was longer on his chin and not fully developed on his cheeks. Otherwise, his face was smooth, his eyes were a light shade of brown, and he locked his gaze on mine.

I closed the door to my office. I pulled one of the guest chairs away from my desk and sat down, gesturing for him to take the other chair. He adjusted the chair to face me and sat slouched.

I reached across to him. "Jed McCain. Deshon, it's an honor to meet you."

He shook my hand and said, "Look, man, this is a waste of time for both of us. I'm here to get my momma off my back."

"Well, we agree on one thing. Your mother is a force we both must reckon with. I'm here to get her off my back, too." I asked, "Do you know why your mother wanted us to talk?"

"Simple, man. She doesn't like my boys—the guys I hang with."

"What does she have against them?"

"Man, I don't know. To listen to her, you'd think they all were gangsters."

"Are they?"

He rolled his eyes. "They're just guys. That's all."

"Let's set them aside for a moment. Tell me something about you."

"Whatchu want to know?"

"How old are you?"

"Seventeen."

"Senior in high school?"

"Junior."

"How's that going?"

"It's goin'."

"What kind of grades are you getting?"

"What's this got to do with my boys?"

"A lot, but just humor me, Deshon. What kind of grades are you getting?"

"What's my momma been telling you?"

"Until a year ago, you were making straight A's, and now you're struggling to pass."

"So?"

"What do you want to do when you get out of school?"

"I don't know. Something."

"Do you plan to go to college?"

"Hell, no. What a waste of time."

"Your mom says you're a math and science whiz. If you went to college, you could write your ticket. Graduates with skills in those areas are in demand, Deshon."

"Ain't no place for a black man." His eyes narrowed as he spit out the words.

"You mean you don't think people will hire a Black man with those skills?"

"No. It means no self-respecting black man wants to work for the man. That's your world, not mine."

"Then what do you want to do?"

"I'm doing what I want right now."

"Which is?"

"Me and my boys, we got some bidnis going."

"What kind of business?"

"We buy and sell stuff."

"What kind of stuff?"

"Everything, man. Depends on what's in demand."

"Your mom says you've been jammed up moving stolen goods."

"Misunderstandings is all. My momma can jump to conclusions."

"She said she had to pull strings to get the charges dropped."

"Wasn't nothing there to drop. We didn't do anything."

"We?"

"My boys. These dudes owed us money. They didn't have it, so we repossessed some property. Misunderstanding, like I said. They'd have dropped the charges anyway."

"Tell me about your boys?"

"Nothing to tell." He folded his muscular arms across his chest.

"How many boys are there?"

"I don't understand what that has to do with anything."

"Your mother seems to think you're involved in a gang."

"They're my friends. Think of us as bidnis partners. We help each other, watch out for each other."

"And are drugs part of that business?"

"Where you getting this shit?" He sat up in his chair, and his eyes narrowed.

"Your mother told me she got you off a marijuana possession beef."

"Again, a misunderstanding. Someone asked me to hold a package for them. I had no idea what it was. I was pulled over for some bullshit violation, and the package turned out to be weed. It wasn't mine."

"Whose was it?"

"A friend."

"Who?"

"Don't matter who. We cleared it up."

"You mean your mother cleared it up."

"Listen, man. I don't know what you're trying to drop on me, but I didn't need no help from my momma. She needs to stay out of my bidnis. I don't need her help. She has her head so far up the White man's ass, she has no idea what's going on with me."

"And what's going on with you?"

"My people have tried this equal rights bullshit, and we're still Black people in a White man's world. There's nothing in your world I want, man. Nothing. My boys and me can take care of ourselves."

"Who's the leader of your boys? Is it you?"

"Ain't me. One of these days, though."

"Who's the leader?"

"I ain't a snitch, man."

"If you're not doing anything wrong, why do you feel like you need to conceal his name?"

"That's just something you don't need to know is all."

"Deshon, let me give you some advice."

"I don't need your advice, Chief."

"I'm going to give it to you anyway. I can assure you, you and your boys are already on the radar of law enforcement, and your mother has run out of favors she can call up should you and your boys have any more misunderstandings with the law. Over my twenty years in law enforcement, I watched scores of boys spend years in jail and even lose their lives going down the path you have your feet on right now. If you continue on this path, I can guarantee the next misunderstanding you have with law enforcement will be one your mother will be helpless to remedy."

Deshon Johnson stood, his eyes defiant. "Are we through here?"

"We're through for now."

I stood, opened the door and let Deshon pass. As he disappeared through the office to the employee entrance, I knew with certainty he and I would talk again.

Johnson appeared at my door. "How'd it go with Deshon?"

"Not like I'd hoped, Sergeant. Not like I'd hoped."

"That boy got a will of iron."

I asked, "Where do you think he got it?"

"I'm guilty." She paused for a moment, collecting thoughts and measuring words. "That boy is headed for big trouble, McCain. What do I do?"

"You keep doing what you're doing. You keep trying to reach him."

"What if I fail?" She took a few steps and sat in the chair vacated by Deshon. "What if he gets himself into some real trouble before we can get through to him?"

"Kids the age of Deshon think they're invincible, until they aren't. Something will happen to cause him to confront that reality. When he reaches that point and he's forced to face himself, which way he chooses to go often depends on how you brought him up. Another cop explained it to me this way. Let's assume kids have an internal tape recorder. As they grow up, parents, as they interact with their children, are continually recording on those tapes. Sometimes kids don't start playing those tapes back until they're on their own, or some event occurs which causes them to dig deep and to play back those recordings. You've been a good mother to Deshon. You may not see it now, but the recordings you've made in him, the example you've set for him, will work to his benefit."

"I hope you're right. I pray you're right. I hope he comes to his senses before something awful happens."

"Me, too."

"Thanks for talking to him."

7

It was nearly four o'clock when Downs came into my office without knocking and perched herself on the edge of a chair in front of my desk. She hooked an errant lock of her red hair over her ear.

"I checked county records, and Sally McCoy's condo is owned by High Seas Securities. They have a Cayman Islands address. I did some checking on the internet, and I can't find out anything about them. It's a shell corporation."

"Cahill may be able to help. Maybe his folks can find out who's behind it."

"I obtained a warrant to search the condo. I'm holding on warrant for phone and financial records until we finish our search of the condo."

"Chief?" Martha Johnson called me from the doorway. "It's the mayor."

"Give me a minute," I said to Downs, "then we'll run out to the condo."

Downs left the office, and I answered the landline on my credenza.

"AJ"

"He fired you?" AJ had a gravelly, booming voice.

"Yes, this morning."

"It says in this email the reason has to do with a violation of an agreement he had with you. Is this true?"

"In a manner of speaking, I guess it is."

"What in the hell did you do?"

"AJ, now isn't a great time to talk about this."

"Okay, I'm not AJ I'm the mayor of this godforsaken place, and I want to know what the hell is going on."

"Can we talk about this tonight? When I get home?"

"Damnit, son, I want to know why."

"AJ, I can't answer your question without creating twenty more. I have a search warrant to process, and when I get home, I'll answer all your questions."

"This won't stand, Jed. I have the council behind me on this. If it comes down to it, if we have to choose between Jarret and you, Jarret is gone."

"I appreciate that, AJ. You must promise me you won't do anything until we talk."

"Tonight, Jed. I mean it."

"Tonight, I promise."

Downs must have been outside my office door because as soon as I hung up the phone, she stepped in. "I'm ready when you are."

Downs and I found the condo building manager, who let us into the unit after we presented the warrant. Inside, there was no sign of Chad Belford. There didn't appear to be anything missing. The unit looked just as it had earlier in the day.

We did a quick walk-through. There were three bedrooms, a master suite and two smaller bedrooms with their own bath. McCoy had converted one of the bedrooms into an office, and the other must have been where Belford bunked. The bed was unmade, the door to the walk-in closet was wide open and a light inside it remained lit.

Downs and I agreed to start with the bedrooms. I'd take the office, and she the master suite.

The spotless office was furnished with two white leather easy chairs and a desk. Like the living area, the exterior wall was solid glass looking west out over the Indian River. The three other walls were light gray and adorned with what looked like expensive oil paintings depicting aquatic scenes. The tile floor resembled weathered light gray planking.

The ultra-modern L-shaped desk, like the furniture we'd seen earlier, was made of glass and white leather. There was a PC workstation on the smaller leg of the L, and in the center of the desk sat a MacBook Air laptop connected to an external hard drive. Both machines were powered down. Also on the desk were a blotter, a white gooseneck lamp, a silver letter opener and a penholder with a white Monte Blanc fountain pen resting at a forty-five-degree angle. Under the desk, below the PC, sat three short filing cabinets. I tried the drawers, but they were all locked. I turned on the PC and the laptop and found they were password protected.

I walked into the kitchen and started opening drawers, looking for a set of keys to unlock the file cabinets. Then it occurred to me that there was no sign of car keys. I called Johnson and asked her to search the Department of Motor Vehicles database to see if Sally McCoy was a registered owner of a vehicle. When she told me she wasn't, we tried Victoria Rockwell. When nothing came up by that name, I asked her to try High Seas Securities.

"Bingo," Johnson said.

"What kind of a vehicle?" I asked.

"Mercedes, E-class Cabriolet. ."

"Only one vehicle?"

"Yep."

"Get all the details and call all the impound yards, police and sheriff's departments and see if we can't find that vehicle. I need the car keys, Johnson. That car has a tracking system of some kind. See if you can run it down. Call me when you find it."

I walked into the other bedroom, and there was nothing except furniture. The room had been picked clean.

I walked into the master suite, which had floor-to-ceiling glass on one wall and a side view of the ocean. Downs was in the walk-in closet, which was the size of my entire house. In the closet, bolted to the floor, was a small safe the size of a mini-bar refrigerator.

"We're going to a need a locksmith to get into that," Downs said as she flipped through evening gowns of every imaginable color and description. The closet looked like a boutique: shoes organized on racks by size and type, built-in dressers, a dressing table with makeup mirrors and lighting that would rival any television studio.

"You find anything?"

Downs pointed to a small section of the closet holding men's clothing. There were suits, dress shirts and dress shoes, none of which seemed to fit what one would expect a surfer like Belford to wear. The suits were of European design, Italian perhaps, and the shoes were from Spain. When Belford had mentioned there might have been other men in her life, it hadn't occurred to me that another man might be sharing Sally McCoy and the condo, too.

"Did you find any identification in the suits that might tell us who the mystery man is?" I asked.

"Nothing. Not even lint, but there are tags on them that would show someone sent them to the cleaners."

"Hold on that. I'm going to have Torres, and her folks come over and scour the place. After they sweep and print everything, call your folks and have them bring a truck and hand trucks to haul these file cabinets and computers back to the PD. Then you can get someone to open the safe. After Torres finishes, have your folks track down the cleaners."

"Anything else?"

"We don't have her cellphone either," I said. "I'm hoping when we find her car, we'll find her phone."

"What if we don't find it?"

"She may have backed up her files or paired her phone with her laptop. From the looks of her office, she was organized. Maybe she'll be organized enough to have recorded passwords somewhere."

"Does anyone do that anymore?"

I didn't say anything.

"Now I know your secret," she said with a smile.

"You call Torres, finish up in here, and I'll check the kitchen and living area."

I went through every cabinet and found nothing untoward. There was a well-stocked bar that could accommodate a large party. In the kitchen, someone had filled the refrigerator with things you would find on the outside aisles of a grocery store. While the spaces were appointed with expensive furnishings, there was no clutter, nothing out of place, and save the office in the bedroom and the safe in the master suite, there was nothing that would shed light on the mysterious life of Sally McCoy.

When Torres and company arrived, Downs said she wanted to stay behind until Torres finished, and she would supervise the inventory and loading of files and computers to maintain chain of evidence. She told me she had someone who could open the safe that evening, and one of her people would come and pick her up when they finished. She promised to call me when she wrapped up.

8

I stopped by a Publix supermarket on beachside and picked up a ready-to-bake pizza and two cold six-packs of Yuengling beer. On my way to the house, I called AJ and told him that as soon as I took a shower and cooked the pizza, I'd call him.

Just as I was coming out of the shower, Johnson called me.

"They found the car. You were right about the tracking device. It was parked in short-term parking at the Daytona Beach Airport."

"Call Torres and a locksmith. Tell her to look for a cellphone and have her go through the car. She'll have it towed back to her shop."

"Why would the car be at the airport?"

"Someone wanted the car out of circulation for a few days."

I dressed, called AJ and set the small table in the kitchen with plates and utensils.

AJ knocked on my sliding glass door near the kitchen at the back of the house. He was very thin, bald and suntanned from boating. He had bushy, expressive eyebrows, a gaunt face and ears too large for his head.

"Hey, Mr. Mayor. Come in."

He looked at the table and said, "Don't you want to eat out on the dock? The sunset is awesome."

"Isn't it too hot?"

"No, and the breeze is amazing."

I put the pizza in the box it had come in and carried it out to the dock, while AJ carried two bottles of beer. We sat on the bench with the pizza between us. He lifted his bottle in my direction, and I touched mine to his.

"To better days." AJ swallowed almost half the bottle in one pull.

I had put the beer in the freezer before I showered. It was cold and refreshing, and I needed it.

I repeated, "To better days."

The cloudless sky was on fire from the retreating sun.

"All right, spill your guts," he said, and chomped down on a piece of thick-crust pepperoni.

"Were you in the military?"

"Yes."

"Were you an officer or enlisted man?"

"Corporal, Marines, Vietnam."

"What's your understanding of chain of command?"

AJ thought about it for a moment, chewed and swallowed a bite of pizza, and said, "It means I report to one person, and I have people that report only to me."

"Let's say for discussion that someone other than the person you report to starts giving you orders and doesn't communicate that with your superior officer."

"That would create a problem."

"How?" I asked.

"Well, I guess for starters, it would create confusion."

"How would the person you report to feel about someone else giving you orders?"

"If he was a Marine, he would be plenty pissed off."

"In the military, you either follow chain of command or lives can be lost. If the guy you reported to found out someone else was giving you orders, why would he be upset?"

"I guess because someone was undercutting his authority."

"Good. We're on the same page. Do you remember Grizzle?" I asked.

"Of course."

"Who did he report to?"

"Jarret."

"Did Grizzle follow chain of command?"

"I've never thought about it."

"Jarret told me Grizzle ignored him and often went around him to the council."

"Ah huh," AJ said.

"When he went over his budget through mismanagement, he would go around Jarrett to the council and get more money. Since Grizzle had friends on the council, he could ignore Jarret. Is that correct?"

"Yes, I guess it is. I haven't ever given that any thought, but yes, he would come to us, and we would let him off the hook."

"What did that do to Jarret's authority over Grizzle?"

"It undercut it."

"Good. When Jarret interviewed me," I took a swig of my beer, "he said he wanted a chief who'd follow chain of command. He wanted a chief who wouldn't go around him to the council. I promised him I wouldn't do that."

"And you haven't."

"I'm not so sure. Remember I mentioned to you months ago that I felt like the city should have its own crime scene unit?"

AJ turned the bottle of beer up and drank the rest. "And I went to the council and proposed we study it."

"And that left Jarret in the dark. I hadn't discussed it with him."

"I thought I was helping you, Jed. You were so low after Sarah James died, I'd have done anything to lift your spirits."

"I know, AJ. I get it. Jarret doesn't, and that's the point."

"I have the votes to reverse the termination, if that's what you want."

"What would my relationship with Jarret be like if you did?"

"There wouldn't be a relationship."

"Correct."

"I'm sorry, Jed. I guess I've stepped in it."

"Jarret feels that because of our friendship, you can't be impartial. He feels our personal relationship will interfere with his ability to do his job."

"Do you want me to talk to him?"

"I don't know, AJ, I broke a trust between him and me. I'm not quite sure how to fix it."

"What was his solution?"

"You and I sever our relationship."

"How do you feel about that?"

"I won't do that. We need to find another solution. I do know this—Jarret is a fine city manager, and the city is fortunate to have him."

"I can't tell you how sorry I am, Jed. I should have talked to you before I went to the council."

"You did what you thought was right. No apology needed. We will figure something out."

We finished off the pizza and drank beer in silence, each to our own thoughts.

If there was any way for me to remain chief, I had to restore Jarret's trust without forfeiting my relationship with   AJ.

9

After AJ left, I sat on the dock and finished another beer as the last traces of the sun disappeared behind the horizon in shades of pink and purple. I regretted being honest with AJ about his culpability in Jarret's case against me. He took things like that to heart. He was a man of honor, though his generation had shown him little of it when he'd returned home during the Vietnam War. AJ was in city politics for selfless reasons. He had told me his success as a banker came from his relationships with the people in the community. He felt it was a duty to give back to the community through his service to the city.

I had no doubt AJ's motive was to help. It bothered me that he felt compelled to apologize for actions that sprang from a pure heart.

My cellphone rang. I pulled it out of my pocket and looked at the lit screen. It was Downs.

"McCain. You won't believe what I found in the safe."

"Try me."

"It was filled with drugs and cash."

"How much cash?"

"I'm guessing, since I haven't counted it all. It looks like a hundred grand, maybe more."

"Drugs?"

"There are several kilos of heroin and enough painkillers to start a pharmacy. There must be several hundred prescription bottles filled with OxyContin, fentanyl, Dilaudid and ecstasy. There has to be one hundred-thousand dollars' worth of drugs in there. I found a ledger in the safe that appears to document transactions, but it's all in code. It will take someone smarter than me to figure it out."

"Did you open the file cabinets or the computers?"

"My folks came and grabbed them an hour ago. They're locked up in evidence until I can look at them in the morning."

"Did Torres find anything?"

"Her team went through the place before we pulled the files and computer equipment. The condo looks like a black dust storm went through. They lifted a ton of prints. Besides things belonging to the victim, they found a toothbrush, floss, hairbrush and personal items that appear to belong to a man. They were in one of the drawers in the master suite. Maybe there's a match to the men's clothing we found. From the DNA we found on the brushes, we might find out the identity of our mystery man if he's in the system. Torres is going to process the dry cleaning tags for prints and trace. I took pics of the serial numbers, and I'll have my folks run down all the dry cleaners in the area for a match."

"Did Torres find anything in the car?"

"It had been wiped clean. No keys. She found a cellphone. It had fallen between the center console and driver's seat. Can't get past the passcode, though."

"Have you touched anything in the safe?"

"Just enough to take a quick inventory."

"Did Torres process the safe?"

"No, she left before the safe technician arrived. I wasn't sure our guy could open it, and I didn't want to hold her."

"I hate to bother Torres again, but she needs to process the safe for prints tonight. I don't want to leave that evidence in the condo, and I don't want it handled until Torres processes what you found. With that much cash there, you'll want to account for the money in Torres' presence and both of you sign the evidence slip. I don't want to give anyone the opportunity to point a finger at anyone."

"Agreed. She won't be happy about having to come back out. The good news is she lives in Coronado Beach. At least she won't have to drive far. Once Torres is done, I'm done for the night."

"Good job, Downs. As always."

I disconnected the call, walked inside to the kitchen, pulled three beers out of the freezer, put two in the refrigerator and opened one. I returned to the dock. The onshore breeze rattled the palms in AJ's yard, and the wind caused a light chop on the Indian River. The reflection from streetlamps along Riverside Drive across the waterway made the black water sparkle.

I took a sip from the slushy beer and set the bottle down on the bench beside me. Despite the challenges at work and losing Sarah, it was hard for me to imagine living anywhere else or having any other job. There were parts of the job I didn't like. That was true. But there was something about this job and this place that felt like home to me. I liked the size of the department and the people I worked with. While my removal as chief seemed certain, I was having a hard time accepting that reality. Between AJ, Jarret and me, it was clear we all wanted what was best for the city. There had to be a way to resolve the problem without blowing everything up.

I thought about the people in the department who would qualify to replace me if my efforts to resolve my issue with Jarret failed. Downs and Johnson came to mind. They both had advanced degrees, and, while

Johnson had no supervisory experience, she did have an administrative background. She served as the department's personnel director, oversaw all the policies and procedures and knew the budgeting process as well as Jarret.

Downs had the education and command experience. She was a superb investigator and respected by her peers; even the commanders who outranked her held her in high regard. He just didn't know whether she would have any interest in the job. She was single, and life was simple. Why would she want to complicate it?

While Johnson had the skills, she was not ready for a command

After six months on the job, I understood why Jarret hadn't tapped Hocking or Morris, the two commanders in the department, to fill Grizzle's job. They were leaders, willing decision makers, did an adequate job, and their people liked and respected them, but they weren't chief material. Nor did I think either of them wanted the responsibility. They were in senior positions in the department without having to engage in political gymnastics. The chief was an easy target for those pushing an agenda. In their roles in the organization, they were out of the political line of fire, and their jobs were more secure.

Leslie Downs was right, though. I was not ready to retire. There were times in the last six months when we hadn't been working on a major case that I'd had a hard time keeping focus from boredom.

I finished off the beer with one swallow.

I was sure the McCoy case was a homicide. While we had no clear proof, we had accumulated significant circumstantial evidence. As a former NYPD homicide detective, I was acquainted with every conceivable way one human being could do away with another. As a rookie, I'd been taught that you could always reduce motive to one of the big three: sex, money or power. After twenty years on the job, ten of them as a murder investigator, my experience had taught me the motivation to kill another was much more nuanced. Between means, motive and opportunity, ferreting out motive, understanding why someone would take the life of another, as morbid as it might be, gave purpose to what would otherwise be a gruesome gauntlet.

I had to admit that knowing and understanding were different. I may know the robber of a bodega killed the clerk for the money in the cash drawer, but understanding why someone would take that life for the twenty dollars in the till was a different matter. Understanding was the haunting part of the job; the spirits of the dead visited me at all hours of the night, demanding justice.

In the McCoy case, it was my experience that the weapon of choice for women was poison. Since women lacked the physical strength to take the life of another and disliked the violence of a gun, poisons leveled the playing field. It was less direct and less violent but just as effective. The axiom didn't always hold true. I had worked on several cases in New York where men had poisoned their victims to make it look like a woman had committed the crime. Some of the most notorious political assassinations committed by men had been facilitated with biological agents or ingested or injected radioactive material like polonium.

The cyanide angle was nothing more than a hunch, since we had no concrete evidence to support the theory. Beyond that, we had nothing to point us to a suspect. The fact that we'd identified suspicious circumstances surrounding the case was encouraging to me. We had leads. In too many cases, leads could be elusive.

I had thought about driving over to the condo where Downs and Torres were finishing up their work but decided my presence might delay the end of their day. It will all keep until tomorrow.

10

When I arrived at the PD, as soon as I put the key in the door to open my office, Johnson scurried from her cubicle. She followed me into my office as I opened the door.

"Chief, they have Deshon. They've got my boy."

"Sit down," I said.

We both sat in the chairs in front of my desk.

Johnson's eyes were red from crying. She handed me her cellphone. It was a freeze frame of an elderly White man surrounded by seven or eight young Black men. Deshon was in the back of the circle on the right edge of the screen. A white triangle with a circle around it in the center of the screen showed this was a video. I touched it with my finger, and the video began to play.

The boys surrounded the man. The only recognizable words were "motherfucker" this and "motherfucker" that. One of the boys, who appeared to be the leader, spat on the man and then moved closer and punched the man hard in the face. The man raised his arms to protect his head, but the rest of them began to pummel him with their fists until he fell to the ground. While Deshon didn't throw a punch, he didn't move away from the others either and appeared to yell words of encouragement.

Someone moved in front of the camera so that the person taking the video had to push forward to capture what happened next. With the man on the ground curled into the fetal position, the Black boy who had spat in the man's face started kicking him in the ribs. When the others joined in, the leader brought his foot down hard on the homeless man's arms that were held up to protect his head. When the kicking transformed into a mass stomping, Deshon backed away from the beating with horror written on his face. Though Deshon did not take part in the beating, it was clear he was with the group.

Someone off camera yelled, "Cops," and the boys scattered.

"Where did you get this?" I asked Johnson.

"From a friend at the Daytona P.D."

"The chief? Downs' father?"

"Yes."

"You said they have Deshon. Who has him?"

"Daytona Beach PD."

"Has he been arraigned yet?"

"It's in the hands of the assistant state's attorney. He's giving Deshon the option of testifying against his friends, something he's unwilling to do. They want me to come and talk with him. That's why I ended up with the video. Unless he helps the prosecutor, he'll be arraigned with the rest of them this afternoon."

"Are you going to see him?" I asked.

"Yes, but I want you to come with me."

"Martha, I hold no sway with him. Yesterday when I talked with him, it was clear my advice meant nothing to him."

"It might now."

"Why? What could I say that I didn't say yesterday?"

"That poor man in the video is dead. They took him to the Halifax Medical Center, where he died from injuries to his head. These boys are facing murder charges. Deshon's only salvation is he didn't directly take part in the beating. Since he was part of the group, he can be charged with them if he doesn't testify against the rest of the boys."

"When do you want to leave?"

"The public defender is with him now. They won't be ready for us until ten."

"Come get me when you're ready to go."

Martha Johnson dropped her head and began to cry. "This is my fault, Chief. I failed my boy."

I stood, crouched down and put my arm around her shoulder. "You didn't fail Deshon, Martha. He failed himself."

Johnson sniffed back her tears, gathered her emotions and stood. "I'm praying my boy will listen to us. This is a nightmare, McCain."

She looked at me for a moment and then shuffled out of my office and into her cubicle.

I went upstairs to Downs' squad. It was an open room with old military surplus desks pushed together next to a long window overlooking the PD's parking lot. There were empty temporary folding tables and chairs lined up against the opposite wall, where the joint drug task force met weekly. The computers we'd seized at Sally McCoy's condo were plugged in and sat on one of the empty tables. Next to the table, Downs squatted in front of one of the two filing cabinets we'd seized and fingered the contents of one of the files in the top drawer. She was alone in the room.

She was wearing a long-sleeve aqua-colored button-up blouse tucked into snug-fitting beige slacks with a wide belt and matching low-heeled shoes. She wore her holster for her Glock 22 on her belt in the small of her back. Her badge was attached to the front of her belt to the left of her buckle.

"What do you have?" I asked.

"Quite a bit," she said. She closed the file drawer in one cabinet, opened the bottom drawer in the other and pulled out a red book with a strap that functioned as a lock, like a diary or journal. She stood up and handed the book to me.

"It has all her passwords in it. She made a haphazard attempt to encode them, but it just took a few moments to get into all her devices: the desktop, laptop and cellphone. The file cabinets were easy to open with a flat-tip screwdriver. A little tug and the locks broke. I just started going through the filing cabinets when you walked in. There was another kilo of heroin in the bottom drawer of that one." She pointed to the open cabinet. "I dusted it for prints and found some. Looks like two sets of prints, but I haven't run them yet."

"When Torres went through the safe last night, what did she find?"

"There were prints all over the prescription bottles and the money. She found prints on the plastic wrapping around the heroin. She's processing all the prints she has this morning. She has a lot of work to do, McCain. She must have lifted a hundred prints, not to mention the ones in the safe."

"Did you count the money?"

"Not yet. Torres is still processing it."

"We need to fingerprint Chad Belford and get a sample of his DNA."

"I was waiting until I get through all this," she looked at the cabinets and computers, "but it is on my list."

"Hear anything from FDLE about High Seas Investments and who owns the condo?"

"Cahill hasn't called me, but he wouldn't. He'd call you."

"Tox screen?"

"That I have. Hunter called me and said they found heroin and ecstasy in her system. Nothing that would have killed her. He said if she was a user, it would be infrequent. There were one or two injection marks, nothing to indicate addiction."

"Cyanide?"

"Not in the tox screen. Hunter is waiting on FDLE for analysis of the tissue samples."

"That's wonderful. I can see us standing in front of a jury, testifying that we think there might be the possibility of a poisoning. Without something definitive—"

"He did find elevated adrenalin levels," Downs interrupted. "Maybe it will show up in tissue samples."

"Maybe. The transaction book you pulled out of the safe?"

"Cahill has it. That's your department."

"Do you need help going through any of this?"

"No. By the time I explain what I'm looking for to someone else, I'll be done."

"Call me when you have something."

I walked back downstairs to my office and called Cahill.

"I was just getting ready to call you with a couple of things," Cahill said. "First, a subsidiary of Florida East Coast Holdings owns High Seas Investments. That company has a single stockholder. Her name is Rachel Finch, and she's the spouse of Raymond J. Finch."

"And who's that?"

"Finch was a lawyer but gave up his practice years ago. His business is political fundraising."

"You mean a money man."

"Yep, and from what I've found out from our folks in Tallahassee, this guy is a major power broker. The

78

Democratic Party in Florida doesn't move without Finch's approval."

"He's that powerful?"

"Yes."

"What's he doing owning a condo?" I asked.

"Could be as simple as a personal investment. He could just be renting the condo out."

"Could be? The decedent could be making enough from drugs to pay the freight for the condo."

"You get into her financial records yet?"

"No. Downs was waiting to go through McCoy's personal effects before we went for the warrant. We're still on thin ice here. We don't have cause of death nailed down yet."

"Ah, the other thing I wanted to tell you about. The tissue samples proved positive for cyanide. Looks like she was murdered."

"Or committed suicide."

"Jed, someone had to take her out to that island. She was pregnant. Doesn't sound like a candidate for suicide to me."

"Can you send all the information over on Finch?"

"Just sent it. He lives in Wilbur-By-The-Sea, near the Ponce Inlet Lighthouse. Did you hear any more about your job?"

"Just that my firing went public."

"I heard. If I can help, let me know. We're still interviewing for an agent. I'm holding the job until we find out what happens with you."

"Thanks, Jim. I appreciate that."

I called Downs and Hunter and shared the cyanide confirmation. I asked Downs to set up an appointment to meet with Raymond Finch after lunch. When I hung up with the ME after asking him to finish his autopsy report, Johnson presented herself and told me we needed to go.

The Daytona PD was located east of I-95, just off Mason Avenue. We went through security, and the desk sergeant routed us to the chief's office. Roger Downs stood up from behind his desk. He was at least six-foot-two with a medium muscular build like a bodybuilder and a full head of wild red hair, a puffy round face covered in freckles and penetrating green eyes. His uniform consisted of a short-sleeve white shirt replete with four stars on his collar, campaign ribbons below his nametag and a badge with "Chief" engraved along the top edge, and dark slacks. He had attached his service weapon to his wide black utility belt.

When I had taken the job of chief in Coronado Beach, I hadn't opted for a uniform and all the military trappings that went with it. I'd yielded to the need for a chief's badge and a CBPD ball cap. Beyond that, I preferred casual clothes.

Standing in Downs' office decorated in a military theme with more than twenty years of memorabilia on the walls and shelves behind his desk was a little intimidating.

"Chief McCain." He came around the desk and extended his hand, and I shook it.

"Sergeant Johnson." He extended a hand to her. "I wish the circumstances of your visit were different. Please, sit down. Before you meet with your son, Johnson, I want to brief you and Chief McCain on where we are."

I looked over at Martha Johnson, and she appeared calm.

"First, your son is in an interview room. The assistant state's attorney hasn't charged him yet. In fact, none of the boys have been charged. However, I expect it to happen at any time. We are waiting until we know the role your son will play in all of this.

"The video of the assault leaves little doubt who was involved in the beating. They planned to record the takedown and then post it on their website. Perhaps they saw it as a rite of passage. For the victim, Charley Grant, who was brutally murdered, it was a horrible price to pay. Fortunately, another bystander was also filming the beating with their phone, and through that video, we identified all of those involved.

"We didn't question Deshon until he had a public defender present with him. The assistant state's attorney met with Deshon and offered to waive charges if he testifies for the prosecution. Until now, he has been unwilling to do so. The public defender is with him now and is doing her best to reason with him."

"Why does he need to testify?" Johnson asked. "The video shows who beat that man and that Deshon didn't participate."

"Sergeant, he was part of that group. Even though he didn't land any blows on the victim, he acted or conspired with the others."

Johnson was silent.

I asked. "How would his testimony be of benefit?"

"It goes to intent, McCain. We don't know whether they planned to kill the guy or whether things just got out of hand. Deshon knows the answer to that question. His testimony against the other boys would make our case stronger. Without his help, he'll be charged with first degree murder just like the others and be arraigned this afternoon."

Johnson said, "He's a good boy, Chief, who got involved with the wrong boys."

"That may be the case, Johnson, but if he doesn't help the prosecution, they'll sweep him up in this, and there's nothing anyone can do to stop it. You have your work cut out for you because he's refusing to say anything, much less talk about what happened." He looked at his watch. "And we're running out of time." He stood up, and we followed suit. "I'm afraid you have one chance to convince your son to cooperate. Once he's charged, there's no going back. They wouldn't have given another boy this opportunity. Your connection to this department and me is the one chance Deshon has. I hope you can get through to him."

Downs escorted us to the desk sergeant. We each shook hands with the chief, he wished us luck, and he reversed course to his office. The sergeant accompanied us to an interview room with a sliding sign that said "Occupied."

I knocked on the door, it snapped open and a small Black woman in a beige business suit asked us to come in.

Deshon was sitting on the opposite side of the table, still wearing the same clothes he had worn yesterday when I'd met with him. He looked like he hadn't slept. When he saw his mother, I could see he wanted to cry, but his fierce pride would not allow him.

The table was long on the sides and short on the ends. There were two chairs on either side of the table. Johnson took the one next to her son, and I sat with the attorney.

"My name is Alice Banks. I'm with the public defender's office." Her hair was short, she smelled of perfume, she had long fingernails painted in bright aqua lacquer, and her voice was soft and soothing. "Chief Downs told me he was going to speak with you and brief you on where we are. If Deshon agrees to testify against the others, no charges will be filed against him."

Martha Johnson said to her son, "Do you understand what they're offering you, son?"

Deshon nodded without speaking.

"You need to do what they're asking. They're going to charge you with murder if you don't."

"Momma, I had no idea they were going to kill that man."

"It doesn't matter, Deshon. You were with them. You were part of the gang."

"I didn't do anything. I didn't lay a hand on that guy."

"It doesn't matter, son. They will charge you with the rest of them. With the video of what happened, there's an excellent chance you could spend the rest of your life in jail."

Banks said to Deshon, "That beating was incredibly brutal. I wouldn't be surprised if they sought the death penalty."

"I can't. I won't."

"Why, Deshon?" Johnson asked.

"You don't know these guys. I testify against them, and I'm a dead man."

I said, "They'll all be behind bars. How can they hurt you?"

"Chief, you don't understand. This gang is much larger than the group that did this. This was an initiation," he said. "If I testify against them, they'll come after me and anyone I love. They'll come after you, Momma. I've seen them do it. They'll drive by our house some night when you're on your way home from work, and they'll

83

shoot you right on the street. I couldn't live with myself if that happened."

As Deshon talked, gone was the attitude and arrogance in evidence in our discussion yesterday. All I saw on his face was fear. Whether he decided to testify or not, either option offered horrible consequences.

"How did you get mixed up with these people, Deshon? How in God's name?" Johnson asked.

"I don't know, Momma. I just don't know." Deshon could contain his emotions no longer, and tears streamed down his cheeks.

I said, "Deshon, a man was brutally murdered for no reason. What do you think is the right thing to do?"

"What difference does it make?"

"You've some very hard choices to make. I don't envy you. When I'm faced with tough choices, I always ask myself, 'What's the right thing to do?'"

Deshon didn't say anything.

"Those boys should pay for what they did to that man. It was the most depraved thing I've ever seen. From the look on your face, while your boys brutally beat this man, you were as horrified as I was. I think you know the right thing to do, Deshon. This can't happen again."

Deshon remained silent, tears still flowing.

Martha Johnson said, "The chief is right, Deshon. We can't live afraid. If we don't stand up to these people, who will? They'll keep on doing things like this until they're stopped."

"Nobody can stop them, Momma. Nobody."

"Well, we can try. The police department will offer protection to you through the trial."

"That won't stop them. If they can't get to me, they'll come after you."

"You don't worry about me, son. I can take care of myself. The department will protect me."

I asked the attorney, "Is the state offering witness protection?"

"Not yet, but I can ask."

"Would you do it now?"

Alice Banks stood up from the table and walked out of the room.

Deshon asked me, "Witness protection? Does that mean I'd have to move somewhere?"

"Yes. When you consider all the options, it's the best one. You could go to prison for the rest of your life, or you could stay here, testify and look over your shoulder, or you could start over somewhere else. Maybe one of these days, if all these guys can be put behind bars, you could come back home."

"Deshon, at least I'd know you were safe," Johnson volunteered.

The door opened, and Banks returned to her seat. "If Deshon will testify against his companions and help local investigators with all he knows about the gang, they'll provide witness protection and relocation. They'll also help him finish school and find work. They're insistent Deshon decide now. This will require a legal agreement that you, Mrs. Johnson, will need to sign with Deshon since he's underage."

"Deshon," Johnson said, "I'm begging you to listen to me. Tell these folks what they need to know. How could relocation be worse than being locked in a cell for the rest of your life?"

"Okay, I'll do it, but I'm telling you, they'll come after you."

"That's not your worry, son."

Johnson decided to remain with her son until the attorneys wrote up the deal and they signed it. I asked Chief Downs if one of his uniforms could give me a lift back to the Coronado PD. On my way there, I gave thought as to how the department could provide protection to Martha Johnson.

While I was in New York, gang violence had been evolving and growing more brutal. Even during the height of organized crime in New York, there had at least been some boundaries on how far gang killings could go. For example, the mob had seldom ordered killings of cops. They had recognized the heat that would descend upon them and concluded it was bad for business. Contemporary gangs killed without constraint, and violence was the currency of their business. Cops were no longer off limits. In fact, cops' families were fair game if it served the gang's purposes.

If the gangs in Central Florida had reached this pinnacle, I was unaware of it. I did know from meetings with the other chiefs of police that gangs were a growing problem, and the level of violence was escalating. Whether it had risen to the level feared by Deshon Johnson, I had no way of knowing. I knew because of continuing budget constraints that around-the-clock protection for Johnson would be short-lived, just long enough to get her through the trial, but after that...

It was clear I needed to know more about the development of gangs in our community and, as a community, we needed to do more to remove the incentive for them to put down roots.

11

"This is preliminary, McCain," Downs said. "I made a quick pass through the computers and files and just browsed everything. Until I dig deeper, I can only generalize what our girl has been up to."

"Just tell me," I said.

"And I still have to get her financial records."

"Downs, what do you have? I won't hold you to anything."

"There are three activities she was engaged in, all of them illegal: prostitution, extortion and drug trafficking. The parties she organized for people tie all these illegal activities together."

"Give me an example."

She guided me to one of the tables where McCoy's desktop computer sat idle. Downs moved the mouse, keyed in a passcode, and navigated to a webpage with a provocative picture of the victim. Above the picture was Victoria Rockwell's name in an elegant cursive font. Below the picture, it said, "Enjoy a romantic evening for two with model Victoria Rockwell."

Below was a menu listing: Images, Contact Victoria, References.

Downs clicked on Images and scrolled through a variety of modeling shots, all with McCoy wearing skimpy swimwear or lingerie.

Under References, there was one paragraph after another lauding Rockwell and the good time had by all without mentioning sex. All the names listed under the references were first names.

Contact Information listed a single telephone number.

"I found boxes of business cards with her picture, her name, Victoria Rockwell, and her website address. Each box had a different web address. I'm guessing she recycled websites often to avoid detection. From everything I see, she used the parties to troll for johns. She seemed to be very selective, fishing for the right candidates to blackmail.

"Again, I've a lot of files to go through, but on her desktop, there are compromising pictures of clients, and when I did a cursory scan of her emails, I found back and forth regarding extortion. At this point, I have no idea how large her client list is or how many people she might have had on a string."

"The drugs?" I asked.

"The parties were underground affairs, held at the homes of rich clients. She supplied the entertainment, drugs, rental furniture and catered food, and managed the invitation lists."

"Who was supplying her with the drugs?"

"I don't know, McCain. I looked through her cellphone, and she called several numbers frequently. Once I get the phone records, I'll have more to go on. Some of the numbers have names attached to them. 'Dude,' I'm guessing, is Belford. There were numerous calls to him. 'Daddy' is another name, which shows up often. I don't know whether that's her father or a euphemism."

I said, "I have a feeling Chad Belford was involved in her business much more than he told us. Run him down. It's time we had another talk with him."

"What if he doesn't want to talk to us?"

"Let's get a warrant for felony possession of narcotics. Give him the choice: he can either talk with us, or we charge him."

"What's next?"

"I want your attention devoted to going through all of this as well as her financial records. Now that you know what you're looking for, get your squad to help you. Since Jim Cahill's folks found Raymond Finch, I want Cahill to go with me when we interview him."

"What would a Democratic fundraiser have to do with the likes of Sally McCoy?"

"That's what I want to know. Good work, Downs. Keep digging."

I walked down to my office. As I passed Johnson's desk, I hoped her time with her son would produce good results for both of them.

I called Cahill.

"Jed, Torres and company have been working all morning on the prints they lifted from the condo. They still have a lot of work to do, but she had a hit on one of the prints. You need to sit down."

"All right."

"William Trent."

"Trent, like Congressman, seventh district Trent?"

"One and the same. His prints were in the master suite bath. We'll find them all over the condo when Torres finishes running everything."

"No kidding," I said. "He must have been in the military for his prints to be in the system."

"Marine Corps. He served in the Gulf War. He was a major when they discharged him and a Medal of Honor recipient."

"I'm assuming the personal items we removed from the condo belong to him?"

"Yes, the prints were from his toothbrush."

"We'll have DNA as well."

Cahill speculated aloud, "Maybe his DNA will match McCoy's child."

I filled Cahill in on what Downs had found and gave a summary of McCoy's various enterprises.

"Pretty soon we'll need a program to keep up with all the suspects," Cahill offered.

"Have you any DNA results for McCoy's baby yet?"

"No. Maybe later today. Perhaps first thing tomorrow. I put a rush on it, but these things take time."

"I was going to interview Raymond Finch. With Trent in the picture, I'm not sure I want to tip our hand until we have more on him."

"Before you climb that tree, Jed, we better have some solid evidence."

"Do you think there's a connection between Finch and Trent?"

"I'd bet a year's salary on it."

"Do you think McCoy could have been blackmailing Trent?" I asked.

"From what you've told me about the pattern to McCoy's business, it doesn't fit the profile. It looks to me like Trent and McCoy had a relationship. The toothbrush in the bathroom doesn't fit the pattern with the other men. Did you say there were dry cleaned suits in the condo? That sounds like they were shacking up together."

"If he knew she was pregnant, it might be motive for murder," I said.

"I think we're getting ahead of ourselves, but it doesn't seem farfetched."

"William Trent. I'll be damned."

Cahill offered, "Let me have my people snoop around the financial connection between Raymond Finch and Trent. If memory serves, he may have even been Trent's campaign manager, but I can't be certain."

"As soon as the DNA from McCoy's child is available, we need to match it from the toothbrush and hairbrush found at the condo."

"As soon as I get off the phone, I'll put a rush on it."

"What about the ledger we found in the safe at the condo?" I asked

"It documents drug transactions between McCoy and her supplier. The codes relating to date, type of drug and dollar amount were easy to break down. The only reference to the supplier was the letters DB. She was a smart cookie. My people feel the ledger was evidence that McCoy could bargain with if law enforcement caught her. With the ledger, she could sell out her supplier and use the information in exchange for immunity. Smart. There are only a couple of dealers in Daytona big enough to supply her. Leslie Downs is on the Drug Task Force; she would be a better source than any we have. My time would be better spent on the financial connection between Finch and Trent."

"You heard about Johnson's son?"

"Yes. Chief Downs and I are good friends. He's doing everything he can to help. He can only go so far."

"He seems like a square shooter."

"They don't get any better, Jed."

12

I called Downs to get Chad Belford's telephone number, and I told her we were going to hold on interviewing Raymond Finch and why. I informed her that while she was working on the files and computers, I was going to interview Belford again and run by the cement plant and talk with Patrick McCoy, the victim's father. I asked her if she had obtained a warrant for a DNA sample from Belford. She said she had.

While I waited for Downs to bring the warrant and a mouth swab kit to me, I called the number Downs had for Belford; I got a recording saying the number was no longer in service. I called campgrounds and RV parks, working my way down the East Coast, until I found him registered at a small park in Melbourne. I called a surfboard manufacturer who told me that when Belford wasn't working for them, he was at Bay and Shore Paddleboards just outside of Melbourne.

I grabbed fast food and drove an hour south. The factory was in a large, rundown metal building in an open field west of the interstate. The dirt road leading off the main highway had a shell base, and plumes of white dust rooster-tailed behind my car. When I found the building, there were several cars parked nose-first around a single white metal door with a Bay and Shore sign stenciled above it. A concrete block leaned against the door to hold it open.

As I approached the entry, a brisk breeze flowed out from the interior of the building. The air smelled of resin, epoxy and acetone. Inside, built into the opposite wall were three large fans that sucked in outside air and exhausted it through the entry door. There were a number of stands with paddleboards in various stages of completion. I walked through a double door to the right. Behind it was an open room with a dozen foam blanks on stands. Belford, with his long hair tied in a ponytail, hovered over one board, spreading what appeared to be yellow-tinted resin over the fiberglass cloth that covered the surface of the board. He wore a respirator over his mouth and nose. Music blaring from a boom box drowned out the noise of the fans in the next room. The chemical smell was overwhelming. I covered my mouth and nose. When Belford looked up from his work and caught sight of me, he started.

I yelled to him over the music, "We need to talk."

He yelled back to me through his respirator. I could barely understand him. "I have to finish this, or the board will be ruined. Give me ten minutes."

With my ball cap and badge, my cop-ness was apparent. As I walked back through the factory on my way out, the workers turned away from me as soon as they recognized I was a cop and feigned absolute focus on their work. From a door on the back wall, a forty-something man wearing a dust mask came out and approached me. His head was shaved, and he wore a goatee.

"Can I help you with something?" The look on his face was one of deep concern. He wore cut-off sweatpants, a sleeveless T-shirt and old black Converse basketball shoes covered in foam dust and resin. A tattoo covered his right arm from his shoulder to his wrist.

I held out my hand. "Chief McCain from Coronado Beach. I'm just here to talk with Chad Belford."

The man brushed his right hand against his shorts and shook my hand. "He in some kind of trouble?"

"And you are?"

"Jacob. I own the place."

"No. I just have a few questions to ask him."

"This about his girlfriend? He told me this morning about what happened."

"I can't discuss that with you."

"Chad's a good guy, Chief..."

"McCain."

"He's been laminating surfboards for me for a couple of years. He does good work, too. All the guys in the shop kid around with him and call him Superlam. He's very talented."

"That's good to know," I said. "How often does he work for you?"

"We're a small builder. I have a full-time laminator, but during the summer months, when orders are heavy, Chad fills in for us. It varies by the time of year. Right now, I have about twenty boards for him. Several of the board builders in the area use him as well, two here in Melbourne. Would you like a tour?"

"No, I'm good. I don't want to keep you from your work. With all the boards piled up, looks like you're pretty busy right now."

"Yes, things are a little crazy. Good... Then I'll get back to my work. If I can help, let me know."

I walked outside and called Downs.

"What do you have for me?" I asked.

"Belford was an accomplice in the extortion scam. I have text messages between McCoy and him to prove it. I just started going through McCoy's phone, but I'll wager he's involved in all the rest of her enterprises."

"His cellphone has been disconnected. I'm sure it's gone."

"Are you going to bring him in?"

"It depends on what he has to say and what else you find."

Belford walked out the factory door, pulling his respirator off and wiping his hands with a paper towel.

"I have to go," I said to Downs.

"I told you everything I know, Chief McCain." Belford took the paper towel and wiped considerable sweat from his face.

"We both know that isn't true. What can you tell me about McCoy's businesses?"

"You mean Vicky's?"

"Yes."

"I told you about them. She was a model, and she organized events and parties for people."

"We found several kilos of heroin in her safe and a cache of prescription painkillers and ecstasy. What do you know about them?"

"Nothing, I swear."

"You're aware the parties she hosted were drug parties, and she was the supplier?"

"No."

"And I suppose you know nothing about her call-girl business and the people she was blackmailing."

"No, I don't."

My cellphone rang. It was Downs. I asked Belford to excuse me and stepped away from him.

Downs said, "I just heard from Torres. She finished running all the prints from the condo and safe. On the heroin and other drugs, McCoy's prints were on the H, the bundles of cash and bottles of pills. Her prints were also on the block of H I found in the filing cabinet. There were prints for a Demarcus Brown, a dealer in Daytona, including the block I found in the file cabinet. Brown has priors for distributing. Then there was another set of prints found all over the condo, and the drugs and money. They aren't in the system, but they belong to Belford."

I ended the call and turned to Belford.

"I'm afraid you're coming with me, Mr. Belford. You've a lot of explaining to do."

"I told you I had nothing to do with anything."

"Your prints are all over the drugs and cash. We have text messages tying you to extortion. We have evidence of another man sharing your condo with a woman you say you're in love with. We haven't pieced it all together yet, but you're involved up to your eyeballs. And this morning we have confirmation that someone murdered your girlfriend. The more we dig into this, the better you look for it."

"I didn't kill Vicky." He threw the respirator he had in his hand to the ground. "I want a lawyer." He avoided looking at me and paced back and forth. "Where are you taking me?"

"The police station in Coronado Beach. Get in the back."

"And if I refuse?"

"Then I cuff you and put you in the car. Your choice. Now turn around."

"Why?"

"I'm going to pat you down."

"All I have is a cellphone."

"What happened to your old one?"

"It quit working."

"Raise your arms."

I patted him down from shoulders to ankles. The only thing in his pocket was his phone.

"Pull your cellphone out of your pocket, please."

I examined it and handed it back to him.

"You'll need this to call your attorney. It would be nice if they were there by the time we reached the PD. It would save us all some time."

I walked to the rear door on the driver's side of the cruiser, opened it and waited for Belford to fold himself into the back seat, and I closed the door. A metal screen separated the front and back seats.

When I jumped in the car, he said, "You're making a huge mistake. I loved Vicky. I don't know who did this, but it wasn't me."

He was silent on the hour drive back to Coronado Beach. He made a call to someone and said he was in a bit of trouble and asked if they could recommend an attorney. He then hung up and dialed another number. He explained that they needed to meet him at the PD. Then he said to me, "It will be two hours before my attorney can be there. She's in court right now."

I tried to question him several times, but he refused to answer. When we arrived at the PD, it was late afternoon. I put Belford into an interview room and posted a guard. On the way to my office, I told the desk sergeant to expect an attorney, and I wanted him to let me know when she arrived.

I passed Martha Johnson's cubicle, and she was just placing her purse and a packet of papers on her desk. I ducked in to check on her.

"Are you done?" I asked.

"No, we're just beginning. It took five hours to get an agreement with the state. They were giving us a hard time about witness protection. The assistant state's attorney didn't think the gang was big enough to warrant the state funding the protection. If it hadn't been for Chief Downs, who convinced the assistant state's attorney that Deshon's help was invaluable in getting the gang situation under control, they wouldn't have gone for it. He reminded the assistant state's attorney of a recent case where this particular gang had made an attempt on the life of an arresting officer in another matter, one they were still investigating."

"Now what?"

"We have the agreement signed, and Deshon is still being questioned by the assistant state's attorney. They'll put him up in a safe house under guard until the trial. They won't even tell me where they have him. Chief Downs assured me they'll take good care of him."

"And what about you?"

"I haven't given it a thought."

"You're staying with me."

"I can't put you in the middle of this, McCain. I won't do it."

"We'll run by your house, get some of your things."

She shook her head stubbornly. "No, we won't."

"Why don't you like my house? I know it's not a palace."

"Stop, McCain. I can take care of myself."

"Until we know what this gang of losers is going to do, I want to at least put a detail outside your house."

"No, I don't want you to do that. Please, now, let it be."

"Why, Johnson? Deshon seemed certain the gang would retaliate. After they're arraigned this afternoon and Deshon isn't among them, they'll know he's been turned."

"McCain, in my neighborhood, police cars are as welcome as the plague. I keep to myself, and I don't make a big deal out of what I do for a living. It's better that way. Now let it be. I can take care of myself."

"What if the cars were unmarked?"

"Give it a rest, Chief. Please."

I left Johnson at her desk and went upstairs to check Downs' progress. She had covered all the folding tables from the Drug Task Force with organized stacks of paper. Two of Downs' detectives sat in front of McCoy's laptop and desktop computers, scanning files. Downs was sitting at her desk in the squad area, typing on her computer.

"What do you have for me, Downs?"

"Let's begin with the extortion. From everything I've learned, the parties she hosted were the principal way she scouted for marks. She did extensive background checks on the men she targeted; the financial records investigation she did on these men were as good as any we do. She was very selective. Between compromising photos, emails and text messages, I can find nine men she has blackmailed over a seven-year period, ten if you include her father. There were no compromising pictures of him.

"The extortion began with her father when she was nineteen. She blackmailed her second mark when she was twenty-one, and the paper trail is sketchy. The other eight were over the last three years. In the photos taken of McCoy in bed with each of her marks, it's the same bed, and the furnishings don't match anything in her condo. One of the pictures shows a window in the background. There are buildings outside from which, with analysis, we may be able to identify the building's location.

"With each mark, McCoy gained confidence, and with it she raised the extortion amounts. I only have records on the last eight men, but her third victim coughed up forty thousand in two installments. She would hit them up for the first payment, wait a few months and then hit them again. The extortion amounts increased with each victim. After they made the second payment, she left them alone. From our last victim, she extorted eighty thousand, and she'd just tried to nick him for another eighty when things went sideways, and she increased it to one hundred thousand."

"So, all of them could be potential suspects."

"The older marks paid their dues, and quite some time has passed. Before her current mark, the last guy she nailed was about nine months ago. There's been no further correspondence. Her current target is the person who'd want to harm her the most."

Downs pushed up from her seat, crossed the room to one of the stacks of paper on the folding tables and came back to her desk. She handed me three sheets of paper. "These are copies of the emails passed between them. Notice his response after her second extortion attempt."

I scanned the note. Halfway down the thread, there was this response: *You better hope I don't find you or you're going to be one dead little bitch.*

She responded by increasing the amount of blackmail to one hundred thousand dollars.

I said, "The girl had some big ones. Do you know who these men are?"

"One was the former mayor of Coronado Beach, our own David Parker. He was number four or five, I think. Some of the other faces looked familiar to me, but I can't put a name to them. I have email addresses on all the men except her father. I have a cellphone number for her current mark. I haven't had a chance to run it down. I'd say the last man she blackmailed had about one hundred and eighty thousand dollars of motive."

"Let's find him."

"All the money in the safe appears to be drug related, and after FDLE helped me figure out the coding on the ledger, the amount of money in the safe tracks with what's outstanding on the ledger. But there are some exchanges between DB and McCoy that indicate all may not have been rosy between the supplier and distributor."

Downs pushed herself up and went back over to the folding tables for some more documents. She returned with what appeared to be printed screengrabs of text messages.

"The telephone number of the text message was stored in her contacts as DB. In summary, although they're coded, the messages document pickups and cash exchanges. From looking at the ledger, it looks like she was moving about a million in drugs per year. I have no idea what kind of money she was making. Everything looked routine until this last series of texts."

She handed me another text message from McCoy's computer. *Word just reached my ears you're buying from someone else. I find out that's true, I'll bury your skinny little ass in the ground, and you'll be sucking air through a straw.*

McCoy answered it with: *Whoever told you that is a liar.*

The text message was dated four days ago.

"Any evidence of her buying from someone else?" I asked.

"None I could find. I did find records for two Cayman Island bank accounts. It was in the book that had passwords and passcodes in it. The account numbers are there, but the passwords aren't. It will take someone with a higher pay grade to get access to those accounts."

"Call Cahill."

"I already did. He's working on it."

"How much cash did she have in the safe?"

"Just over three hundred thousand."

"I'll have Johnson start the seizure paperwork."

"Demarcus Brown won't be happy." Downs explained, "With the ledger she kept and the supply we found in her apartment, Brown will have a lot more than the three hundred grand to be unhappy about." She smiled ever so slightly. "I saved the best for last. William Trent. Not only do we have his prints, one of my guys tracked down the cleaners who cleaned the suits we found in the condo. Not only are they his, the clerk there identified Trent from a photograph as the person who dropped them off and picked them up.

"I've also found emails and text messages between McCoy and Trent. From what I can tell, they've been in a relationship for a while. I still have many emails I haven't read, but I have some recent ones that talk about him divorcing his wife."

"Any mentions of her pregnancy?"

"If there are, I haven't seen any. That's what I have my people doing right now. They're reading through all the text messages from 'Daddy' and reading every email."

"You said McCoy was blackmailing her father."

"Yes, but the emails are very vague. I could find nothing that would indicate the reason," Downs continued. "This one email says if her father doesn't pay her, she'll expose what he did to her. 'Everyone will know.'

"It sounds like incest, doesn't it?"

"In the case of Sally McCoy, like her mother said, there seems to be no bounds for evil. The line of folks who had a reason to kill her gets longer by the minute."

"You folks finish up here. I'm going to see if Belford's attorney has arrived. If the timing works out, I want to catch Patrick McCoy before he gets off work."

"If you're going to question Belford, I want to do it with you."

13

I asked the officer outside the interview room if Belford's attorney had arrived.

"About ten minutes ago."

I opened the door. On one side of the conference table, Chad Belford sat huddled with a woman whose back was toward me. I walked around to the opposite side. The woman with Belford turned and gave me a polite smile. She was in her mid-thirties, of medium height, trim, and had long black hair. She stood to introduce herself.

"Hi, I'm Ashley Rand. I'm representing Mr. Belford. And you are?"

"Jed McCain, chief of police."

She sat down again, and I continued standing.

"Before we get started, Chief McCain, have you charged my client?"

"No. At this stage, we just want to question him about the murder of his girlfriend."

"Is my client a suspect in that murder?"

"Perhaps. It depends on how our session goes. We believe Mr. Belford engaged in several felonious activities with the decedent. Mr. Belford told us he was in love with Ms. McCoy, and we've learned she had engaged in prostitution, extortion and drug trafficking. Your client lived with and had a sexual relationship with Ms. McCoy. She also shared the condo and her bed with another man, who paid the bills for the place. Mr. Belford doesn't have an alibi for the evening someone murdered Ms. McCoy. Given Ms. McCoy's intimate relationships with many different men, we feel Mr. Belford may have had a motive to kill the woman."

Rand took notes on a steno pad lying in front of her.

I continued, "We have evidence linking Mr. Belford to drug trafficking. We also will prove your client conspired with the decedent to extort money from men with whom she had prostituted herself. We also believe Mr. Belford, upon learning the decedent was pregnant..."

"Let's slow down, Chief."

Belford belted out, "I've told you people, I didn't kill Vicky. I loved—"

Rand put her hand on his. "You will not say another word, Mr. Belford." She said to me, "This sounds like a fishing trip, Chief McCain."

"Ms. Rand, your client is in serious trouble. We'll charge him with trafficking, delivery and sale of narcotics. He may also be charged with conspiracy to commit extortion, with evidence we already have, and more we expect to collect later today and tomorrow. He is now our only suspect in the murder of his girlfriend, until we can question him further. Without his cooperation, we'll charge him with her murder."

"And why should he talk to you? It seems to me if you have enough to charge my client, you would have done it."

"Sally McCoy, with material help from your client, was engaged in several criminal enterprises. The focus of our investigation is the murder of Ms. McCoy. If your client, as he claims, didn't kill her, then the better we understand their criminal enterprises, the better the chances of us finding her killer. If he's cooperative, we've some flexibility in the crimes we will charge him with."

"I need to talk with my client. Could you give us some time?"

"When you're ready to talk, call me on my cellphone."
I pulled a card out of my wallet and handed it to her.

She gave me a polite smile, and I left the room.

I called Downs and told her I'd delayed Belford's interrogation, and I drove to the concrete plant west of town to interview Patrick McCoy.

Southeast Volusia Materials sat on a spur of the Florida East Coast Railroad. It was a hundred-acre site that was both a quarry and concrete plant. I drove through the main gate, where I showed my badge and told the guard who I wanted to see. He made a phone call and then gave me directions to the dispatcher's building, where the drivers checked in and out, and pointed me toward the concrete plant, a conglomeration of silver towers, tanks and pipes.

I parked at a single-story building. It was near quitting time, and there was a trickle of concrete trucks returning to the yard. One at a time, the drivers parked in a line along a fence and walked to this building to turn in paperwork and check out to leave for the day.

I walked inside, spoke with the first official-looking person in the building and told him I wanted to talk with Patrick McCoy. The man said I had just missed McCoy and pointed at him walking across the parking lot to his pickup truck.

I jogged across the lot and caught up with McCoy as he was unlocking his 1990s vintage truck.

"Patrick McCoy?"

He looked at the badge on my belt. "This is about Sally, isn't it?"

McCoy was in his fifties. The skin on his face, neck and arms were wrinkled and sun-damaged. For a truck driver, he was bone thin. Rust-colored hair curled out from under his ball cap, and his eyes were a deep green. His face was pockmarked from acne.

"I just have a few questions," I said. "Would you mind?"

"Didn't you already talk to the missus?"

"I guess I wanted to get your version."

"You think I'd have anything more to say than she has already told you?"

"I was hoping you would."

"Sally was a piece of work. What was your name?"

"McCain. Chief McCain."

"I'm afraid I can't offer you any more than what my wife has already told you."

"You don't have any idea who'd have wanted to kill her?"

"No."

"We've been going through Sally's files and computers, and it seems she may have been involved in blackmailing men who she may have had a sexual relationship with. We have emails and text messages that go back several years. Would you happen to know anything about that?"

He looked down at his shoes and ground a circle into the dirt with the toe of one of them. He didn't respond.

I continued, "We found correspondence. Your daughter was blackmailing you."

He looked up at me, the rims of his eyes red. "And you're thinking I might have killed her?"

"I haven't drawn any conclusions, Mr. McCoy. I'm just trying to find out what happened. Was she blackmailing you?"

"She tried."

"Would you care to explain?"

107

"Could we sit in the truck? I've been in this sun all day."

We climbed into his truck, and McCoy started the engine and flipped the air conditioning to max-air.

He began without my encouragement. "My wife told me about her conversation with you, and I know you've some idea how sick this girl was. My wife believes she was pure evil. She has no idea.

"When Sally was seventeen, she wanted this Mustang convertible in the worst way. We refused to give her the money for it. Then she tried to steal the money from our savings."

"Yes, Mrs. McCoy told us about that."

"What she didn't tell you is one night after my wife went to bed, Sally offered to have sex with me if I'd give her the money for that car. She even began to take off her clothes."

"What happened then?"

"Nothing happened. Not a damn thing. I slapped her and told her to get the hell away from me."

"And?"

"Then she tried to steal the money from us. Two years later, I received this email from her threatening to expose me for raping her the night she tried to seduce me. The letter didn't come right out and say it in those words, but there was no getting around what she meant."

"What did you do?"

"That night, I shared it with the missus. I told her what happened. You see, I know my daughter. I knew how she was. When Sally sent me that email, she'd just hit her mother up for money, and when Verna wouldn't give it to her, Sally threatened me. I also refused to give her the money. I told her mother already knew about her sexual advances and I had nothing to hide. I never heard any more from her."

"That's the last time you talked to her?"

"Yes."

"Do you have any idea who'd have wanted to kill your daughter?"

"My daughter was a beautiful girl. She was stunning. She would cut your throat, however, if she thought it would benefit her. I hate to say that about my own flesh and blood, but it is true. Do I know who'd have done it? No. Although I could understand why they'd want to."

"Your wife mentioned your daughter was a sociopath. Was she ever diagnosed with that disorder?"

"Yes. By the time she was twelve years old, we knew something wasn't right with her. She was a compulsive liar, uncontrollable, selfish to an extreme. It cost us money we didn't have, but we took her to a string of psychologists without success. Chief, Sally was smart, brilliant in fact. Her I.Q. scores were off the charts. Counseling was nothing more than a mental game to Sally; it was an amusement. In the end, my wife and I gave up trying to help her and did the best we could just to survive life with her until she was of legal age. She was a living nightmare. An absolute nightmare."

In his voice, I sensed both deep sorrow and immense frustration.

"How did she die, Chief?" he asked.

"Poisoned."

"You think someone poisoned her, or did she commit suicide?"

"Do you suspect suicide?"

"She's threatened it several times. I always thought she did it for attention or to get her way. When I heard she'd died, I thought about it."

I pulled a card from my wallet and handed it to him. "If you think of something, call me. I'm sorry about your daughter."

"I appreciate that. In many ways, it's the final chapter in a very ugly story. I'm glad it is over."

14

As I was heading back to the PD, I received a call from Ashley Rand.

"Chief McCain," she said.

"Ms. Rand."

"Could we meet somewhere and discuss Mr. Belford's situation before you question him?"

"That's a little unusual, isn't it?"

"After my discussion with him, I've a better sense of what's going on. If I had a better idea of where you want to take this, I might be more inclined to encourage him to answer your questions."

"Where?"

"Are you familiar with Outriggers?"

"Yes."

"Could we meet there in ten minutes? At the bar?"

"All right."

I parked my unmarked cruiser in the parking lot and found Rand seated on a stool at the outdoor bar. Happy hour patrons filled the place. The din from people trying to talk over each other was deafening. The seat next to her was empty.

"I'm glad you came," she said.

I could barely hear her. "Is there some place quieter?" I asked.

The bartender must have heard me and suggested an outdoor seating area next to the bar with chairs around a fire pit.

Rand slipped off the stool, grabbed what looked like a martini and led the way. She was about five-seven and looked out of place in the bar in a business suit and heels. We found two chairs away from the crowd and sat facing the marina. A college-age girl took my draft beer order and departed.

Ashley Rand was attractive. She had a thin face, dark features and a small mouth sporting fresh red lipstick.

"Is this better?" she asked.

"Much. What did you want to talk about?"

"Right to the point! All right. Are you familiar with codependence?"

"Yes. It's a one-sided relationship where one person is addicted to the other."

"People with codependency often form relationships that are destructive. The picture I'm getting is that Belford was in love with or addicted to Vicky, or whatever her name was. She used sex to control him and constantly threatened to end their relationship if he didn't do things for her that were often illegal. If you understand anything about codependence, you'll understand he was incapable of killing her. He might have killed for her, but he couldn't have killed her."

I offered, "We can prove another man was living in the condo on occasion. I'm not at liberty to go any further than that, but it must have driven him crazy that McCoy was sleeping with someone else under the same roof. If he loved her as you say, it had to grate on him to take part in her prostitution scheme to extort other men."

"I can assure you it was tearing him apart. It was torturous."

That would make sense to me. That's what makes this such a sad story. He was in love with this girl, she treated him like shit, and he was powerless to do anything about it."

"Let's assume you're right. Your client is still important to me because he has been in the middle of everything. What he knows could be helpful in finding the killer."

"After my discussion with him, I'm convinced he has material information which would help your investigation. And if you charge him and we go to trial, I'm convinced the codependency is a mitigating condition that would get him off."

The explanation she offered made sense to me. The more I learned about the bizarre relationships surrounding Sally McCoy, the more I believed it would take someone with deep emotional issues to stay connected to her.

"What do you propose?"

"In exchange for his full cooperation, I want a plea deal where he'll confess to his part in all this woman's enterprises, with probation and no jail time."

"You know I can't agree to that. It's up to the assistant state's attorney to make the call."

"Will you support it?"

"Yes, if he answers all our questions."

"All right. Do I have your permission to approach the assistant state's attorney on this? I want his assurance we have a deal before Belford tells you what he knows."

"I'm all right with that, but I want to see the agreement before you and the assistant state's attorney sign off on it."

"Agreed. We aren't going to get this done before morning. Will you release my client with my assurance I'll have him back to you for questioning in the morning?"

"I can't do that, and I don't think it would be wise for you to put your hide on the line for him. As soon as he learned McCoy was dead, he moved out of the condo, disconnected his cellphone and left town. It took a bit of work to track him down. If we let him loose, we may not find him again. When he has answered all our questions, we have what we need from him and he fulfills his obligations under the agreement we put together, then, if there are no other pending charges, we'll kick him loose."

"Fair enough." She picked the olive out her martini and put it in her mouth. "I understand you're new to the job."

"Six months." I withheld that Jarret had fired me.

"You're from New York."

"You checking up on me, Ms. Rand?"

"Don't flatter yourself. Your accent."

"Yeah, I guess that's a dead giveaway."

"What do you think of Coronado Beach?"

"I like it. Humidity can be oppressive at times, but it could be that way in New York, too. You're a transplant, too?"

"Nope, born and raised here."

Our server returned, and Rand ordered another martini, making it obvious she felt comfortable stepping over the line from professional to personal.

Rand said, "Tell me about you."

I smiled and asked, "This have anything to do with Belford?"

"Not a thing. Call it feminine curiosity."

"Not much to tell. I retired from the NYPD after twenty years and found a position here."

"Double dipping?"

"Yep. Half the retired NYPD police force is working in Florida on a second retirement. That sounded good to me."

"Married?"

"More feminine curiosity, Ms. Rand?"

"Call it whatever you want. We aren't going to get to know one another if we don't ask questions."

"Is that what we're doing, Ms. Rand?"

"Call me Ashley."

I said, "Divorced, no children. You?"

"Divorced. I have a daughter, thirteen. May I call you Jed?"

"Sure."

She shifted in her chair to face me. She brushed a lock of hair off her smooth forehead.

"I feel comfortable with you, Jed. I don't know if you feel that chemistry or not." The server dropped her martini off and placed it on a small table next to her chair. Rand continued, "I'd like to get to know you better, but as long as I'm involved in this case, It wouldn't be appropriate. Perhaps, after we conclude our business with Mr. Belford, we could have dinner. How do you feel about that?"

"I'd like that."

"Do you mind if I ask why you divorced?"

"My ex left me for an attorney she worked for."

"Now that's a coincidence. My husband left me for a cop. A male cop."

"Let me guess. Your ex was an attorney."

"And my law partner. Soon to be ex-partner."

"That sounds complicated."

"I was crushed at first, but it would have been much worse if he'd left me for another woman."

"Is the cop with the Coronado PD?"

"Yes. Can you believe it? He left me for a younger man." She giggled at her own joke. She lifted her drink off the table and consumed half in one swallow. "Jed, I need to go. I need to call the assistant state's attorney and get the paperwork going on Belford." She stood, finished off her drink and said, "I'll have the agreement sent to your office before eight in the morning. If everything is acceptable, you can begin questioning as soon as I can go over it with Belford and have him sign it."

Ashley extended a hand to me, which I shook, and she gave me a warm smile. "Thanks for meeting with me, Jed." She walked through the bar and disappeared down the walkway toward the parking lot.

I did feel the chemistry Ashley Rand had mentioned. She'd surprised me with her willingness to tell me how she felt, but it was welcome. The way she expressed herself was matter-of-fact and honest. It marked the first time since Sarah James' death that I had a flicker of interest in another woman. I had to admit to myself, I wanted to pursue it.

15

As I was leaving Outriggers, my cellphone rang. It was Downs.

"I'm done with McCoy's files and computers, and I'm starving. Have you eaten yet?"

"I'm just walking out of Outriggers. Where are you?"

"I'm across town, down toward Bethune Beach. I'm in a small house off A1A that sits up on stilts. Some of Torres' people are here lifting prints."

"I'm confused, Downs."

"Sorry. When I dug into McCoy's financial records, I noticed regular payments to a property management company. They were for the house we are searching now. This is where McCoy filmed her victims. Do you want to have dinner or not?"

"J.B.'s Fish Camp is near you, isn't it?"

"Two blocks away."

"I'll meet you there in fifteen minutes."

J.B.'s Fish Camp had a boat launch, fish house and T-shirt shop, and sat on Mosquito Lagoon and the Indian River. It was a favorite of locals, but it was overrun with snowbirds during the winter months. I had eaten in the restaurant before, preferring the outside tables overlooking the water. The host showed me to a picnic table that had a clear view of the setting sun. A backlit thunderstorm appeared as though its edges were on fire as the cell moved in front of the sun.

"So, how did you manage to get this impressive table, McCain? When I come in here, I always get stuck with a table on the side with no view or inside the restaurant." Downs sat on the bench opposite me.

Without responding, I turned back toward the sun, easing below the horizon and the lightning veining inside the clouds of the small storm near it. I turned back to Downs, who had her chin propped on her hand, contented to watch the remnants of light shifting from deep orange and yellow to purple. The offshore breeze played with the locks of Downs light red hair, and the last vestiges of sunlight reflected off her blue eyes.

Somewhere inside the restaurant, someone turned on strings of lights that hung from the canopy above us, pulling Downs back from the far-off place she had drifted. The air smelled of salt, fish and food cooking in the kitchen.

She caught me looking at her, dropped her hand from her chin and smiled. "You ever wish you didn't have to deal with so much death?"

"Yes. Especially in New York, when I had to deal with it every day."

"How did you handle it? And don't give me that 'someone has to do it' bullshit."

"I don't think I ever 'handled' it. There were times I didn't handle it at all."

"What do you mean?"

"An eight-year-old girl is killed in a drive-by shooting. She was walking on the sidewalk and had nothing to do with it. Or a young woman is beaten to death by her boyfriend who's high on meth. You don't 'handle' those at all."

"It seems like all we deal with is the slime life has to offer. You ever feel that way?"

"This case getting to you, Downs?"

"When Mrs. McCoy told us her daughter was evil, I didn't believe her."

I told her about my discussion with Patrick McCoy, that his daughter had tried to seduce him, and when that didn't work, she'd blackmailed him.

"Why does that surprise me?" she said with sarcasm.

"What did her mother say? Sally would do anything to get what she wanted."

"Well, I have some things for you." Downs leaned forward, put her elbows on the table and clasped her hands in front of her.

Just as she started to tell me, our server came to the table to take our drink order.

Downs asked, "Are we on or off duty?"

"Off," I said.

We both ordered margaritas.

"Before you start, I want to fill you in a little more on Belford," I said. "His attorney convinced me he's not Sally McCoy's killer. She thinks he'll provide us with information helpful to our case. In exchange for his cooperation, we will plead him out with no jail time. The paperwork is in the works now. We can interrogate him in the morning."

"Who's the attorney?"

"Ashley Rand. Do you know her?"

"Of course. She's ripped me to shreds on the stand several times."

"So, what do you have?"

"Rand talked you into a plea deal?"

"She didn't talk me into anything. I knew Belford didn't kill McCoy the moment we told him she was dead. He's up to his neck in her prostitution and extortion scheme, and her killer is most likely someone she tried to extort. Without a deal, Rand wouldn't let him answer our questions because of self-incrimination. Finding McCoy's killer is more important to me than prosecuting Belford."

"I agree. I don't know what she had on him, but he was her gofer."

"You said you were done with McCoy's files and computers. What else did you find?"

"I told you about the men she'd blackmailed," Downs said. "Well, the last one is James Hunt. He's the one who threatened McCoy. I found him by running down his email address and cellphone number. He's the owner of Southeast Volusia Materials."

"That's where Patrick McCoy works."

"Yep. Sally McCoy threatened to send the pictures to Hunt's wife and the *News-Journal* in Daytona. The threatening email and her upping the amount of blackmail occurred the week before her murder."

"What else?"

"The phone number labeled 'Daddy' on her iPhone was a prepaid cellphone from Walmart that has been disconnected. I'm pretty sure it's Trent's phone, but we can't prove it unless we find it in his possession."

"What did you find in the house you searched?"

"Still searching. FDLE's people are still there processing the scene. It definitely was the place where McCoy recorded all the sex tapes and pictures. The master bedroom had a one-way mirror on the wall. Behind the mirror, someone drilled a hole into the wall that opens into a closet in an adjoining bedroom, and they mounted a video camera on a tripod to capture everything."

"Any prints yet?"

"I brought a copy of Belford's prints to the home. We lifted prints off the camera, and they matched his. As soon as they run the rest of the prints, they'll let us know.

You don't think Belford had anything to do with McCoy's murder?"

"If any one of the men in McCoy's life had turned up dead, he would be my first suspect. He loved her. Why, I don't know, nor do I understand. He said it himself, 'I'm a sick shit.'"

"What if McCoy's baby is his?"

"I don't think it changes anything, other than making this all the more bizarre," I said.

"So, let's walk through what we have. If Belford didn't do it, do you like her father for it?"

"He said she tried to seduce him, and when he wouldn't buy into it, she tried to blackmail him. He refused, filled his wife in on the plot and Sally moved on."

"I like Trent myself, if the baby was his. Let's assume he was just shacking up with her, a woman on the side. He's married; I confirmed that this morning. If McCoy turned up pregnant, and it was his child, the scandal would ruin him. What if she was playing him as she had played the other marks? If she threatened to expose him, it might be motive enough for him to kill her."

"And there's still her drug supplier, Demarcus Brown," I said. "McCoy used people. What if her relationship with Brown went sideways? What if she was blackmailing Brown with the ledger? She's extorting everyone else. Why not him?"

"It would fit her profile, but I didn't find any evidence to support it. It does, however, provide a viable explanation on why she kept the ledger." Downs mused, "I have to give the girl credit, she had some guts. She was playing with fire and either didn't understand the risks or didn't care."

"Belford said she was fearless."

"Well, she screwed the wrong person, and it got her killed."

Our server came bearing two drinks. Downs and I both ordered fish and chips.

"Heard anything more on your job?" Downs inquired.

"No, nothing. I've been a little wrapped up today with this case."

"I can tell you no one in the department is happy about it."

"That surprises me. I haven't been here that long. I haven't even been introduced to everyone."

"You have no idea how bad things were under Chief Grizzle. No one respected him. He was out for himself, and everyone else be damned. Can't you just do whatever Jarret wants you to do? We can't lose you. I think most everyone is willing to come down with a case of the blue flu if you think that might help."

My cellphone rang just as I was about to tell her how much I appreciated her comments. It was a frantic Martha Johnson. "Someone just firebombed my car!"

"Call it in. We're on our way." I told Downs, "We have to go." I stood up, reached into my pocket for cash and dropped two twenties on the table.

"What's going on?"

"Someone just torched Martha Johnson's car."

We ran to the parking lot.

"Leave your car here," I said. "I want you to come with me."

We left J.B.'s with lights and siren and raced to the old section of town. When we turned down Johnson's Street, there was a maze of police and fire vehicles, with blue and red lights bouncing off the houses. Downs and I ran from the car toward a smoldering late-model car charred beyond recognition in Johnson's driveway. The smell of burned rubber and plastic wafted from the black mess. Johnson was standing next to a fire department rescue truck, but she looked okay. The fire department was putting hoses away and preparing to leave.

"You okay?" I asked Johnson, who was standing with her fists on her ample hips next to a patrol person.

"Yeah, I'm all right. I hate to lose that car, but I'm good."

I was going to ask her if she still felt she didn't need a security detail, but I thought better of it. "You thinking the gang did this?"

"I know they did this."

"How'd it happen?"

"I was watching the news, and I heard glass break. I ran to the front door; my car was on fire, and I just caught the taillights of a car turning at the end of my street."

"Can you make the car?"

"No. All I saw were taillights, and even then, I couldn't tell you anything about them."

"Maybe one of your neighbors saw something."

"In this neighborhood, no one sees anything."

"Let's put some uniforms on the street. Maybe someone will come forward."

"You're wasting your time."

"These are your neighbors and friends."

"I'm a cop, McCain. I'm on my own."

"You can't stay here tonight. Why don't you stay with me? It isn't fancy, but I have a spare room."

Downs spoke up. "Martha, I have plenty of room."

"No offence, McCain, but I think I'll stay at Leslie's. I don't want to leave until I get my things out of the house. They may come back, and I have some personal things I don't want to lose."

"I'll stay and help," Downs offered.

"Take my car, Downs," I said. "Give me your keys, and I'll have Corporal Davis drive me out to J.B.'s and get your car. We can swap in the morning."

"Deshon can't know about this, McCain," Johnson said. "If he knew, he wouldn't testify."

"There's no press here," I said. "We can keep it out of official records."

"Well, the neighbors won't talk about it." She chuckled grimly.

Downs handed me her keys.

At J.B.'s, as I was leaving the parking lot in Downs' car, Cahill called me.

"Jim, Martha Johnson's car was firebombed tonight," I said.

"They didn't waste any time, did they. Did you call Chief Downs yet? He should be made aware of it."

"You're right. I'll fill him in."

"I have some news. I was thinking about a drink, too. Sandy is out for the evening with her mother."

"Do you have the DNA results?"

"I do, but I need a drink and someone to drink it with."

I was exhausted and already feeling the effects of the drinks I'd had earlier. I had Belford's interrogation in the morning, and I needed to know whether he was the father of McCoy's baby before I met with him. It would surprise me to learn Belford would be any more than a puppet on the end of a sexual string.

Over the past six months, Cahill has become more than a colleague. These impromptu meetings when his wife Sandy had plans had become the glue that bound us together, so I agreed to meet him.

16

We agreed to meet at a restaurant with a tiki bar on Rose Bay, halfway between Coronado Beach and Daytona. The place was a ramshackle, but it was on the water, and the drinks were cheap.

Cahill was sitting at the bar, waiting on me. The bartender, who hadn't shaved in several days and wore his gray hair pulled back into a ponytail, asked me what I wanted. I told him a beer.

Cahill said, "You're not having a Scotch?" It was the drink of choice for our biweekly conferences.

"I've already had a couple of drinks, and I still have to make it home without a DUI. I wouldn't want to get fired from the department."

Cahill smiled. "Right. We wouldn't want that to happen. Anything more on your job? If you have to come to the FDLE, at least I'm the devil you know."

"No, nothing yet."

"You know I want to help."

"I know, Jim, but I don't know what I want to do. If I go to Jarret and cave in on selling my house and severing my relationship with AJ, it puts me in a very weak position with him in the future, and I don't want that. On the other hand, if I do nothing, he won't back down."

"Do you think he's bluffing?"

"No. Not Jarret. I just need to think it through. There's a solution; I just haven't found it. Now, tell me about the DNA results."

Cahill raised his right eyebrow. "The baby's DNA is a match to Congressman Trent."

"Wow."

"That's not all. I was right that Raymond Finch was Trent's campaign manager, but he was also Trent's chief fundraiser. The two are close. They both graduated from the University of Florida, and they were in the same fraternity. When Trent left the service, it was Finch who ran his campaign for the Florida State Senate before he ran for Congress."

"Sounds like Trent wanted a girlfriend and Finch made the arrangements."

"Wouldn't be the first time a politician skimmed campaign funds into a personal slush fund."

I asked, "Is that what you think happened?"

"I don't know. We're looking into it, but quietly. If we go too far, we move into the FBI's turf. Finch is loaded, though. He runs a hedge fund and develops real estate. He could have done all this with his own funds to help his friend have an affair."

"What about McCoy's Cayman accounts?"

"Downs found a username and password. Our people dug into the account. Sally McCoy had accumulated two-point-six million; we're trying to find out from the IRS if she paid taxes on that money. Cayman bank accounts aren't what they used to be. The U.S. Government has agreements with most of the banks there to report large sums stored by U.S. citizens."

I said, "That, along with the cash we found in the condo, will go a long way to funding the city's new crime lab."

"Not if we don't seize it first." Jim laughed. "You ready to interview Finch?"

"I'm thinking we interview Congressman Trent first. If we begin with Finch, two seconds after we conclude discussions with him, he'll be on the phone to Trent, and that would give him time to plan a response. Besides, what'll he tell us that we don't already know? We can place Trent in the condo, and McCoy's pregnancy cinches up their relationship."

"When do you want to do it?" Cahill asked.

"Tomorrow afternoon, after we finish with Belford."

"If you don't mind, I'd like to be part of that."

"I have no idea where this is going, Jim. I'd welcome it." I took a drink from my beer. "What do you know about Ashley Rand?"

"The attorney?"

I nodded.

"She defended a state house representative we'd charged with taking bribes. She cross-examined me— and that is the most charitable way to describe what she did."

"That doesn't answer the question."

"Other than the fact that she's good-looking and tore my ass up on the stand, I'd say she is impressive. She got her client off on a technicality, and we had a solid case. Why are you asking?"

"She's representing Chad Belford, McCoy's boyfriend."

"My impression was she was competent and tough."

"We're going to question him in the morning. She negotiated a plea arrangement in exchange for his cooperation."

"You ruled him out as a suspect?"

"On the murder. On the drugs and extortion, we have him nailed down. I'm hoping he can shed some light on who killed her."

"It's not my case, but I like Trent. He would be at the top of my list."

"A list that's getting longer."

I filled him in on James Hunt and the threatening email he'd sent McCoy before we found her on Disappearing Island. "We also want to talk with Demarcus Brown, the guy supplying her with drugs."

"I want to go back to the beef between you and Jarret. Now, I don't want to lose Torres, but she has been digging into finding federal money to put a crime lab in Coronado Beach. From what she was telling me, it might not cost your city a cent. We were kidding about using the seizure money to fund it—and that might be possible, too, but I think she has dialed into the right programs. You should listen to what she has to say."

"She said she wanted to talk to me about it over dinner."

"And that's bothering you? Jed, she's the biggest flirt on the planet. Don't take any of it seriously. She doesn't mean anything by it."

"And all this time, I thought she was interested in me."

"You and a thousand other guys."

"So, she was pulling my leg about dinner?"

"I don't know, but I can assure you that's as far as it would go. You should talk to her. She's FDLE trained, and she knows her stuff." Cahill raised his glass to get the bartender's attention. "One more thing. You're buying tonight. I bought the last time."

17

It was six a.m. Still in pajama bottoms and a T-shirt, I took my coffee out to the dock. The morning air was heavy with humidity, and traffic across the South Causeway Bridge to my left was beginning to thicken with cars. I could hear the *click-clack click-clack* of tires hitting the expansion joints on the concrete surface of the bridge as cars and trucks passed by.

I thought about the case, the department and what I might do if I didn't find a solution to my problems with Jarret. The hurdle I couldn't get over was the issue of trust between Jarret and me. Yes, I understood his rigid adherence to chain of command, but in a small town like Coronado Beach, where everyone knew everyone, it was impossible for the chief not to have contact with people on the council. And the folks on the council wanted to have contact with him. They weren't trying to pry or go around Jarret. There was just something about having a relationship with the head cop in town. They all wanted to feel a part of what we did. Whether it made them feel safe, they had a morbid curiosity about the underside of their city, or it made them feel good about rubbing elbows with city leaders, they all had found a way into my professional life. This all happened without crossing any of the lines Jarret had insisted on.

I couldn't go into a coffee shop without someone on the council asking me how things were going, or they'd ask about some criminal event they had read about in the local paper. It was in Jarret's interest for me to play the public relations game with the council because those relationships worked for the benefit of all the city employees. If I held to his rigid lines of communication, I wouldn't talk to anyone. That would help no one.

My relationship with AJ was part of a much larger issue. If I caved to Jarret's demands, it would fix the communications issue in the short term, but it would continue to be a problem in the future. The solution was for him to trust me. Yes, I had screwed up and mentioned the crime lab idea to AJ, but in my defense, I had not been asking for his support or action. It had just come up in conversation. AJ had been curious why FDLE did this work for us, and I had answered the question more broadly than I should have. Jarret and I needed to talk again. I knew I only had one shot at getting through to him and I needed to prepare for the meeting.

I had no idea what I'd do if I left the department. While Cahill's offer to work for him was intriguing, working for him would complicate our friendship, and our friendship would complicate working for him. While my pension was decent, living on it alone would be a bare-bones existence. I wouldn't have the funds to fix my house up, which it needed. While buying the ugliest house in an upscale neighborhood had been a good financial call, owning the worst-looking house on the block didn't endear me to my neighbors. I loved the house and sitting out on this dock in the morning. I needed to find a way to stay.

The McCoy case weighed on me. I was sure from everything we'd learned that William Trent was involved with Sally McCoy's death. Call it cop's intuition. I hadn't even met the man, and I had already moved him to the top of my list. An old NYPD detective had told me once that men with high political aspirations who sought positions of power had enormous appetites that came along for the ride. I'd never forget him admonishing me to remember that with power comes abuse, and the greater the power, the greater the abuse. Worse, when the powerful fell, they always tried to take down those who had toppled them. While the NYPD had a special squad to investigate high-profile cases, I worked on my share. In one case, a councilperson had murdered his wife and accused me of planting evidence implicating him. The gun we found was a "throw-down," one where all the serial numbers had been removed. With help from his attorneys and investigators, the councilperson and his investigators planted evidence supporting charges they brought against me and accused me of planting the gun. The NYPD suspended me, and, for a time, PD brass thought the charges had merit. In the end, other forensics proved the councilperson was the killer and exonerated me.

My experiences as a homicide investigator bore the detective's theory out. As I anticipated calling out Congressman Trent, I was mentally preparing for the blowback, which would no doubt come from exposing his secret life with Sally McCoy.

When I arrived at the PD, Martha Johnson followed me into my office. As soon as she sat down in the chair in front of my desk, she burst into tears.

"I went by my house this morning to get some personal items I forgot last night. The front door had been pried open with what looked like a crowbar, and those animals had destroyed the inside of my house. I mean there wasn't one thing they hadn't ruined with a hammer, a knife or acid. Every wall, door, outlet, fixture, window was beaten to smithereens. Nothing was overlooked."

I didn't know what to say. All I could manage was, "Martha, I'm so sorry." I thought for a moment and said, "Let's get a crew out there. Someone must have seen something."

"Downs' people are there now. Uniforms are going door to door, but no one will say a word. Even if they saw something, none of them would risk having what was done to my house done to theirs. Thank God I had snagged the things that meant something to me out of that house last night. And the poor people I'm renting from don't deserve this. I pray they have insurance."

"What time did this happen?"

"My smashed clock in my kitchen said two-eighteen."

"It was good you were with Downs."

"No telling what would have happened if I had been home, McCain."

"Did you call Chief Downs in Daytona?"

"There's nothing he can do without proof or eyewitnesses. We know who did it, but that's not doing us a bit of good." Johnson pushed herself up out of the chair, put her fists on her hips and said, "They aren't going to intimidate me, McCain." She gave me a determined look and walked out of my office.

I resolved to call Chief Downs when I finished my interview with Chad Belford. It was clear Johnson was in harm's way, and with the trial months away, the state needed to sequester both Johnson and her son until the trial was over. After that, perhaps Johnson should relocate as well. I'd dread sharing that opinion with her, but for her own protection, it might be wise.

It was nearing eight-thirty when Downs stopped at my office to accompany me to the interview room.

On my way home from drinks with Cahill, I called her and told her about the DNA results that ruled out Belford as the father. I had also relayed the information about Raymond Finch's relationship with Trent and that Trent was the father of McCoy's unborn child.

Downs told me she'd brought Belford from our holding cell and that Ashley Rand had been with him since about seven-thirty.

When we opened the door to the interview room, Belford was signing papers as Rand flipped over pages and indicated where he should initial and sign. She'd sent me a copy of the agreement before I went to bed. I had agreed with the terms and reiterated that his full cooperation determined whether the deal was valid.

Rand and Belford were sitting on one side of an oblong table, and Downs and I sat in the two opposite chairs. Rand handed me the agreement to show where Belford had signed, and the assistant state's attorney's signature line was blank. The assistant state's attorney would sign with a word from me that Belford had cooperated.

Downs and I had already agreed she would lead the questioning.

Downs began, "First, I want to advise you both that the conversations we're having are being recorded." She began by identifying all the participants by name and gave the case number, time and date.

"Mr. Belford, how would you describe your relationship with Sally McCoy?"

"Vicky, I mean Sally... It'll be hard to get used to that... Sally and I met about six years ago..."

"I'd like to focus on the more recent past, Mr. Belford. At the time of Ms. McCoy's death, how would you describe your relationship with her?"

"I lived with her and worked for her."

"And what did she employ you to do?"

"Anything she wanted me to do."

"Let's begin with her prostitution. What role did you play in that?"

"It would be better if I could start from the beginning."

Downs relented. "Okay, start from the beginning."

"We met at a rave in Daytona. I was trying to sell some ecstasy, and she wanted to know where I was getting it. She told me if I was trying to sell drugs, I sucked at it, and she had a better way. She'd just broken it off with someone and didn't have a place to crash. I offered to let her stay with me. She didn't think much of my place either. She told me if I could get the drugs, she had a way to make a lot of money. Her idea was to organize drug parties. She convinced this rich guy she'd dated a couple of times to host the first party. It was small, and it was my job to get the drugs. I way underestimated the amount of drugs needed, but the party was a success anyway. She demanded I introduce her to my source. And from then on, she handled the drug buys."

"Was Demarcus Brown your supplier then?"

"No, someone who bought from him. Vicky saw the potential of her parties and found a way around my guy to deal with Brown."

"And how long have you been buying from Brown?"

"Five years. I wasn't buying from him, Vicky was. She didn't trust me to do that. She would place an order with Brown, and I'd pick the drugs up and pay for them."

"So, what did you do at these parties?"

"I provided the labor. She would order rental furniture, tables and chairs, and I'd haul them and set them up. She would hire the bands or entertainment, and I'd set up the stages or equipment. She used to tell me she was the brains of the outfit, and I was the brawn."

Downs asked, "So you were business partners?"

"She used to tell me we were, but she ran things."

"Did that bother you?"

"No. Vicky was smart, and she was beautiful. Without Vicky, I'd still be peddling dime bags and starving.

"Did Vicky have any trouble with Demarcus Brown?"

"Constant problems. Brown kept raising his prices, trying to squeeze Vicky out. He wanted to control her parties. They didn't trust each other either."

"Why?"

"She was convinced when she refused to pay more for his product that he was cutting the heroin with quinine or starch. He thought Vicky was reselling his product to other dealers."

"Was she reselling?"

"No, but Brown was convinced she was."

"Did he ever threaten her?"

"Yes. She tried every trick in the book to get around Brown to his supplier. She was too small a dealer to get anyone's attention. If Brown had found out about it...he would have killed her."

"Did Brown and McCoy have any recent disagreements?"

"No, just their normal bickering."

I'd thought when Belford said McCoy was beautiful that it had come out as regret rather than a compliment, and apparently Downs had noticed it, too.

"Was Sally's beauty a problem for you?" she asked.

"When I met Vicky, I had no direction. I was a boat dead in the water. She knew what she wanted and took over. She was amazing. She was beautiful, and she knew it. She used it."

"You're referring to the prostitution."

"That's what it looked like, but it was more than that. Vicky understood the vulnerabilities people have. She knew how to take advantage of them. That's why her parties were successful—because she found a need. People wanted drugs, but they didn't want to troll the streets for them. She created a safe environment for people to hook up."

"When you say she wasn't involved in prostitution, what do you mean?"

"The prostitution thing was a show. She knew the effect she had on men and played it. As these parties grew, it was the rich and connected who hired Vicky to put them on. She would get the list of invitees from her clients and spend days doing research on who she thought fit a certain personal and financial profile. At the parties, she would dress in provocative outfits and flirt with the men she targeted, offering an evening of 'entertainment,' as she used to call it. To the men she approached, it looked like sex for hire. To Vicky, it was all about blackmail; what she charged these guys for sex was peanuts compared to what they'd pay to shut her up."

"And what kind of men did she target?"

"Rich guys who couldn't afford a scandal."

"Like James Hunt?" Downs asked.

"Yes."

"And political figures."

"Yes."

"And what role did you play in this?"

"Vicky and I rent this house down the beach. We rigged the master bedroom with video cameras and microphones. I operated all the equipment and edited the video we used to blackmail them. Vicky decided how much to blackmail them for, and I sent the emails, instructing them where to drop the money, and I made the pickup."

"How many men have you blackmailed?"

"Maybe ten or eleven."

"And how much money would she blackmail them for?"

"It started out small, but I'd guess she's made nearly a million since we've been together. That does count the money she's made from the drugs."

"And how did she pay you?"

"She used to tell me my pay was living and sleeping with her. That aside, she would give me a small percent of everything we made."

"Was William Trent one of the political figures you blackmailed?"

"Who?"

"Congressman Trent."

Belford gave Downs a puzzled look.

"The guy who was living in the condo with you and McCoy."

"Oh, him. Bill."

"Were you blackmailing him?"

"No." I could see Belford's mood change. He sat forward in his chair and looked from side to side.

Downs continued, "Who was he, then?"

"Vicky referred to him as her sugar daddy. She said he was paying for the condo and her car and other things."

"How did the arrangement work? Did he live there with you and McCoy?"

"When he was there, I had to leave."

"Then Bill didn't know about you?"

"No. He didn't."

"Were you ever there when he was there?"

"Yes, a couple of times. Vicky told him I was her computer tech."

"So, she was not blackmailing him?"

"No."

"How would you describe their relationship?"

Belford was silent for several seconds, and Downs repeated the question.

"She wanted to marry him." A darkness descended on him. His eyes narrowed, and he lowered his head. He moved his hands as though he was washing them.

I interjected a question. "You were in love with her?"

Belford looked up at me. "Yes."

Downs asked, "And she was in love with Bill."

"No."

"You said when we first talked to you that McCoy only loved herself."

"She was incapable of loving anyone."

"So, how did you feel about Bill living with McCoy?"

"I hated it."

"Did you know she was pregnant with Bill's child?"

"No. It doesn't surprise me, though. She had her sights set on him."

"You mean to marry him?"

"Yes."

Downs pulled a picture of William Trent from a manila file and laid it on the table in front of Belford. "Is this the man you refer to as Bill?"

He glanced at the picture and didn't hesitate. "Yes, that's him."

"What do you know about him?"

"Only what Vicky told me."

"And what did she tell you?"

"That he was loaded, powerful, and he was her ticket out."

"Out of what?"

"All of it."

"Including you."

"Yes."

I said, "That had to piss you off."

For the first time, Ashley Rand injected herself into the conversation. "This is a line of questioning we agreed not to delve into."

"I want to answer it." Belford looked at Rand for approval.

Rand nodded.

Belford continued. "It hurt more than made me mad. It didn't hurt any more than Vicky sleeping with the men she blackmailed. It didn't hurt any more than watching her whore herself out at the parties we threw. It didn't hurt any more than having to photograph her having sex with other men. She had no concept of right or wrong. She saw the drugs, sex and blackmail as a means to an end."

"And what end was that?" Downs asked.

"Power and money. She craved them like people at her parties craved their next drug score."

"If it hurt so much, why didn't you leave her?"

"I tried. Several times. Like she craved power and money, I craved her, and I couldn't get enough. She knew it and used it. What's worse is I knew she was using me and let her do it."

Downs looked at her notes. "You said she wanted to marry Bill. Do you think she became pregnant to trap Bill into marrying her?"

"I don't know. I wouldn't put it past her. She was secretive about her relationship with him. She didn't hide it. She just withheld information about him and wouldn't tell me much."

"Do you think Bill could have killed her? A pregnancy could have created a problem between them."

"If they were having issues over it, she never told me. Hell, I didn't even know she was pregnant. How far along was she?"

Downs checked her notes. "Two and a half months."

"I had no idea. Could we take a bathroom break?"

"Yes, let's do that," I said. "Downs, show Mr. Belford where the bathrooms are."

Rand said to Downs, "Could you turn off the recording equipment? I want to speak with Chief McCain in private."

Downs acknowledged Rand and escorted Belford from the interview room.

I turned to Rand and said, "When we resume, I want to go back to James Hunt and question Belford about threats Hunt made against McCoy. I also find it strange McCoy's father is employed by Hunt's company."

"You don't believe in coincidence?" she asked.

"No. I've been doing this job too long."

"I thought we agreed you wouldn't question him about the murder."

"We did, and I get that Belford has problems. The curious side of me wanted to know how a man could be so disrespected, emasculated and not want to hurt someone. I agree he's not a suspect, but if it had been me, I couldn't have controlled my anger."

Rand smiled and said, "I'll have to remember that for future reference."

18

Downs brought Belford back into the room.

"We're back recording." She identified all the parties in the room and gave them the time and date. "Mr. Belford, with the exception of James Hunt, did any of the men you and Ms. McCoy extorted refuse to pay the blackmail?"

"No."

"Did any of them call or involve the police?"

"No."

"At the time of her death, were you blackmailing any of the men before Hunt?"

"No."

"And what was the process you followed?"

"You mean the sex part or the blackmail?"

"The blackmail."

Belford sat back in his chair and flipped his long hair over his shoulder.

"We would text a picture of Vicky and the guy doing it. The note was simple. We would send the picture to the guy's wife and the newspaper if the guy didn't pay the amount we wanted. If he didn't text, we would send the information through email. The text would instruct him to drop the money in a storage locker at the bowling alley by a certain time. I'd stake out the parking lot until the drop was made and make sure the guy had left before I went in to retrieve the money."

"And once he paid, what was next?"

"We would wait a while and repeat the process, this time for more money."

"And then?"

"That was it."

"Why only twice?"

"Vicky said if we pushed any harder, we'd push our guys to go to the police. She had this expression, 'Pigs get fat, hogs get slaughtered.' She was right. They paid up, and we didn't have any problems."

"Until James Hunt."

"Hunt was different. After he paid the first payment, he hung around the bowling alley waiting for us to pick up the money. He gave up or thought better of confronting us. He went ballistic when we hit him the second time. I told Vicky I had a bad feeling about Hunt and asked her if she was sure she wanted to blackmail him the second time. She was adamant. It pissed me off since it was me out there exposed. He sent Vicky a threatening email."

Downs pulled a copy of the Hunt email from a folder and handed it to him. "Is this the note he sent to her?"

He read it and shook his head. "I never saw it. She told me about it, though."

"What was her response?"

"She jacked up the amount of the blackmail even higher. When I reminded her of the pigs and hogs thing, she told me Hunt was an exception."

Downs pulled a picture of Patrick McCoy from the file. "Have you ever seen this man before?"

Belford picked the picture up, gave it a look and gave it back to Downs. "He looks familiar, but I can't place him. Who is it?"

"Ms. McCoy's father. Were you aware Ms. McCoy's father worked for Hunt?"

"No."

"Was there anything different in the way Hunt was selected to be blackmailed?"

"No. She met him at a party she hosted. The only thing different was it was some political event, but it was very private. Maybe ten to fifteen people."

"Do you remember who it was for?"

"No. She didn't want me there."

"Then how did you know how many people were at the party?"

"She told me when she gave me a list of drugs she wanted to take with her."

"Do you know who she was working for?"

"No. She didn't tell me, but I have the feeling it was something Bill was involved in or one of his friends."

"And Bill—William Trent—was he ever the target of blackmail?"

"No. At least not that I was aware of."

"Did Hunt make the second installment?"

"No. I checked the locker at the bowling alley."

"And when did you do that?"

"The day before she went missing."

"Was that day the deadline you gave him to make the second payment?"

"Yes."

I said, "You've told us very little about Bill. The guy was living in the same place with you. Surely you know more about him."

The darkness I had seen in Belford's face earlier returned. He turned and looked at Ashley Rand and gave the question thought.

"I didn't want to know about him. I told Vicky that, but she had her sights set on him."

Downs asked, "Between Hunt and Demarcus Brown, was there anyone else who had threatened her?"

143

"No, not that I'm aware of."

"Indirectly?"

"None of the guys we blackmailed were happy about it."

I asked, "If you were making a percentage of what Ms. McCoy was making, why did you continue to work on surfboards?"

"One of these days, I want to own my own factory. I want to make my own surfboards, have my own label. I knew my days with Vicky were numbered."

I asked Downs if she had any more questions. She didn't.

"Mr. Belford," I said, "we've no more questions for now, but, per our agreement, we may have more in the future. You have agreed to testify against Demarcus Brown or James Hunt when a case is brought against them. You have also agreed to testify against anyone else that you had knowledge of who may turn out to be a suspect in this case. You also agreed to remain in touch with us."

Belford nodded. "Can I go?"

"Yes, you're free to go."

Ashley Rand said to me, "If you need to question him further, call me."

Downs and I stood. Rand and Belford did the same.

Rand said to me loudly enough for all to hear, "Could I meet with you in private?" She said to Downs, "Is the taping system still on?"

"I'll turn it off now," Downs said.

When everyone but Rand and I had left, I closed the door. "What's up?"

"Downs did a nice job. She's very bright." Rand was still sitting in her chair, and I sat down across the table from her. She continued, "And she is very attractive." She raised an eyebrow.

"Is this what you wanted to talk about? Whether I'm attracted to one of my subordinates?"

"I'd be curious to know, but no, that's not what I want to discuss. There are two things. One is your dismissal as chief, and the other is William Trent."

"What do you know about my being fired?"

"Just what I read in the *News-Journal* and what I heard from my ex's boyfriend. The word is you're well-liked in the department and you've improved its operation in a short period. I don't understand why they fired you. I just wanted to offer my help if you feel the need. Is this something you want to talk about?"

Rand was sitting back in her chair, hands folded in her lap. Her cool gray eyes surveyed my face. She'd spoken of chemistry the last time we met, and I felt that draw. I connected to her openness and serenity, not to mention her beauty.

"What's your interest in William Trent?" I asked.

"He's a client of Eddy's. Had I known he was a possible suspect, I'd have passed on representing Mr. Belford. It is a clear conflict."

"So, what happens now?"

"We need to talk about it."

"So, Trent is your law firm's client?"

"No. My ex's."

"Now that you know we're pursuing Trent, what happens now?"

"That's why I want to talk to you."

"About your many conflicts of interest?"

"My divorce from Eddy was complicated. Ending the marriage was simple. Eddy came out of the closet, and that was that. What was complicated was the law practice. If we broke up the law firm, we were both afraid we would lose a lot of business, and, in a small town like Coronado, it took years of hard work to build our practice. We decided to take it slow."

"How long have you been divorced?"

"Two years. In that time, I've learned some things, and now I've acted on them. As of yesterday, Eddy and I have separated our law practices. Since the divorce, I've learned a large percentage of our clients would have followed me had I severed my relationship with Eddy. Eddy loves criminal defense work. Of the cases we handled in our practice, I disliked handling criminal cases the most. When we were together, it worked out well because he specialized in one area and I in another. Most of our firm's clients are non-criminal and need the help of a generalist. That's the work I like. So, I've broken away from Eddy to start my own practice."

"Why did you feel the need to confide in me?"

"Because I want to ask you to have dinner with me, and I don't want you to think I've any ulterior motives."

"And Belford?"

"It's pretty simple, Jed. If you agree to have dinner with me, I'll hand his case over to Eddy. If you don't, I'll finish his work for him, and Belford will be my last criminal case."

"I'd love to have dinner with you."

"I was hoping you would say that." She smiled.

"What about the information you learned about Trent and our interest in him?"

"I'll keep it in confidence. Ethics requires me to do that, but as of last night, Trent is Eddy's issue."

"What's your impression of Trent?"

"For all the reasons I just mentioned, I'd prefer we not discuss Trent at all."

"All right, we won't."

"Let's talk about your job for a moment. What're your thoughts?"

"The city manager requires a very rigid chain of command, which I agreed to follow. Unknowingly, I bought a house next door to AJ McFarland, who was a city councilperson at the time. We became friends. The city manager feels uncomfortable with that relationship."

"What happened that warranted your dismissal?"

"I made casual mention to AJ that FDLE did our crime lab work. He asked me why Coronado Beach wasn't handling it. I explained it was financial. It was nothing more than that. A month later, AJ introduced a proposal to study the financial impact of installing our own crime lab. Since I hadn't discussed it with the city manager, he went nuclear on me. Jarret feels I now have undue influence over the mayor, making it difficult for him to supervise and make decisions about the PD."

I then explained to Rand what Jarret required in order to forestall my dismissal.

"That's drastic, isn't it? What're you going to do?"

"I don't know. A solution is elusive. He doesn't trust me, and that's the real issue. In his defense, the previous chief gave him plenty of reason to be leery."

"Chief Grizzle was a buffoon," she said.

"While that may be true, he had relationships with the old mayor and city council that proved problematic to Jarret."

"You like Jarret, don't you?"

"Yes, I've a lot of respect for him."

"Can I help?"

"You're doing it now."

"So, are you having dinner with me tonight?"

"I'd like that," I said.

147

19

I called Chief Roger Downs.

"You heard about Martha Johnson's house?" I asked.

"Yes. Sergeant Johnson called me earlier this morning."

"Any developments?"

"Deshon has been an excellent source of information for us, but we're still in the middle of the investigation. He'll be an excellent witness. We need more hard evidence to put these guys away for a while. We're just not there yet."

"What about the boys who killed the old man Grant? You have Deshon's testimony."

"I know, McCain, but there's more at stake here. Deshon's gang's activities involve racketeering from Ormond Beach to Coronado Beach. The boys involved in the man's death are in the freshman class, just kids. That's how they start them off. We want to take the whole gang down. We're trying to roll them from the bottom up. Deshon Johnson and a couple of other younger members of the gang know enough about the leaders a level above them to put them away. We hope to use this strategy to work our way up through the organization."

I said, "Meanwhile, the gang is intent on taking Martha Johnson out to intimidate her son. She's in harm's way, Downs. We must do something."

"What do you suggest?"

"She needs to be in protective custody as well, and she needs to be relocated along with her son. Her boy isn't even out of high school."

There was silence. I didn't feel the need to break it.

"All right, let me check with the assistant state's attorney. You think Martha Johnson's life is in danger?"

"They firebombed her car. They destroyed her rented house. She told me there wasn't one thing left in her home that hadn't been destroyed. What do you think?"

"I'll work on it. Anything else?"

"Is there a connection between the gang Deshon is in and Demarcus Brown?"

"No. In fact, the opposite. There's a war brewing. The city-boy gang has grown and is encroaching on Brown's turf. Brown runs his operation like the mob, like a business. Brown is organized and operates with a minimum of violence. This city-boy gang operates like a terrorist organization. They're militant, ruthless, violent and fast growing. That's why Deshon's testimony is crucial. This is a cancer we have to kill, or they'll make Brown's organization look like child's play."

After hanging up, I called Lesley Downs and asked her to call Congressman Trent and get an appointment to see him after lunch.

"What if we can't get in to see him?" she asked.

"Tell his people it is regarding Vicky Rockwell, and we will release his name to the press as a person of interest if we can't meet with him."

"All right, but the shit is going to hit the fan, McCain."

"We're as ready as we're going to be. Let's get it over with."

"When you have something scheduled, call Cahill and have him meet us at his office."

Ten minutes later, Lesley Downs called and said Trent would meet with us at one-thirty, after lunch, at his attorney's office in Coronado Beach. Downs said she had called Cahill. I asked her if we were meeting at Edward Rand's office, and she said yes.

As soon as I hung up the phone with Downs, Cahill called and said he wanted to meet for lunch. He suggested that if Downs was going to sit in on the interview with Trent, we should all get together and talk about how we would conduct the meeting. I suggested a restaurant on Canal Street three blocks from the PD. It was also close to Rand's office.

When I hung up the phone with Cahill, Martha Johnson was leaning on the doorjamb to my office.

"You called Chief Downs," she said.

"Yes."

She sidled into the office and plopped down in the chair in front of my desk with a huff. "He called me. He said you suggested any witness relocation involving Deshon include me."

"Yeah, I did. You need to be with your son. He needs you."

"I don't have a choice, do I?"

"No. If it is handled right, we may be able to find something for you in law enforcement."

"I can't believe this has happened to me. If the boy had had a father, this wouldn't have happened, McCain."

I had no response.

"Chief Downs wants me in the same safe house as Deshon while he works things out. They already have a protective detail guarding him."

"That makes sense. At least you'll be with your son."

"Do you want me to resign or quit?"

"No, let's not get ahead of ourselves. You have plenty of leave."

"I have several things I'm involved with right now that I can't drop."

"When can you have them done?"

"By tomorrow. Do you think Downs would mind me staying with her another night?"

"No. And I'll put some uniforms on her house tonight."

"I'll call Chief Downs and let him know. Oh, and Jarret just called. He wants to see you. He said it's important."

Neil Jarret was pacing in front of his desk when I appeared at his door. He ran a hand across the top of his baldhead.

"Have a seat," he said, gesturing toward the small conference table in his office.

I took a seat and folded my hands on top of the table. "What's up?"

"The mayor just resigned!" He dragged a chair away from the table and sat opposite me. He looked at me like it was my fault.

"What? When did this happen?"

"About twenty minutes ago."

"Why?" I asked incredulously.

"You know exactly why."

"I have no idea what you're talking about."

"He told me he quit so you won't have to."

"The law of unintended consequences."

"Did you talk him into this?"

"Listen, Neil. I have no control over what the mayor does. The man has class. I'm shocked he did this, but it isn't out of character. What did he say when he resigned?"

"He said he was an old man, and the job wasn't important to him. He wouldn't be the cause of you losing your position."

"Well, that should solve your problem. I can't say much for the solution, but that's what you wanted, isn't it?"

"No. McFarland is an incredible and supportive mayor. I need him. There are many things the former mayor screwed up that he can help me fix."

"Sounds like you have some things to think about. I have to be in a meeting in ten minutes. Let me know if I can help."

"Are you sure you didn't put him up to this?"

I stood, walked to the door and turned around to face him. "Neil, you need to back away from this. AJ did this on his own. The problem you and I are struggling with is one of trust. And you've no reason to mistrust me."

As I walked away from his office to get Downs and head to our meeting with Cahill, it occurred to me that when we try to control things as Jarret was doing, we discover how little control we have.

Downtown shoppers filled the small restaurant, and as soon as the host seated us, I knew my choice of restaurant was a mistake. The restaurant's owners had jammed tables into every square inch of space, and the din from folks trying to talk over each other made it difficult to hear. Our server took our orders.

Cahill said, "I'm surprised Trent agreed to meet with us."

"He is concerned about publicity," Downs said. "We're meeting in his attorney's office."

"Who's his attorney?"

"Edward Rand," I said.

Cahill looked at me and raised an eyebrow.

I said, "Ashley Rand is defending Belford."

"Are they related?" Downs asked.

"They were married. They're divorced. And as of yesterday, they no longer practice law together."

"Does that mean Ashley Rand will share everything we discussed this morning with her ex?"

"I don't think she'll do that," I said with assurance.

Downs asked, "Who'll take point in the meeting?"

"Jed," Cahill said, "you should handle this. FDLE is just assisting in the investigation."

I turned to Downs. "Do you have all the evidence pertaining to Trent's involvement?"

Downs pulled a file folder out of her backpack and handed it to me. I breezed through it and handed it back to her.

Our food came, and our conversation paused while we ate.

After we finished our meals, Downs asked, "How are you going to handle this?"

"I haven't a clue," I said.

"I get it. How do you interrogate a congressman?"

"Just like anyone else."

20

Eddy Rand's office was a few doors down from the restaurant. It was on the second floor, above several shops along Canal Street. A glass door off the sidewalk with Law Firm emblazoned in gold letters welcomed us to a stairway. At the top of the stairs, a receptionist greeted us and accompanied us to a conference room. A waist-high long window offered a view of the street below. A moment later, two men entered the room.

I recognized William Trent from the pictures Downs had given me. He was rugged, handsome and presidential-looking, with dark hair graying at the temples. His eyes were so green, I wondered if he was wearing tinted contact lenses. In his forties, with a square build, he looked like the war hero he was.

Eddy Rand introduced himself as Edward. He was in his late thirties and had a full head of white hair and brown eyes. His body was lean and his suit expensive.

We all shook hands and found seats around the table.

Rand began with, "It is my understanding you're here to discuss the death of Victoria Rockwell. Is that correct?"

"Yes," I said.

"Is my client a suspect?"

"Not at the moment, but that depends on how this interview goes."

Rand said, "I've advised my client not to answer any questions, that you'll submit your questions to me in writing, and we will provide an appropriate response. However, he insists he had nothing to do with her death and wants to help in any way he can. He's agreed to this interview voluntarily. If I feel your questions are inappropriate, I'll advise my client not to answer them."

"Congressman Trent," I said. "Describe your relationship with Victoria Rockwell."

"I was in love with her."

"Were you having an affair with her?"

"It was much more than that, Chief McCain. We were going to be married."

"Aren't you married now?"

"Yes."

"Did your wife know about Ms. Rockwell?"

"Yes."

"How long has she known?"

"Since we found out Vicky was pregnant."

"And when was that?"

"Three weeks ago."

I was stunned. I looked at Downs and Cahill, their faces filled with the same astonishment.

"How long have you been in a relationship with Ms. Rockwell?"

"Over a year. We met at a political fundraiser she'd organized for my campaign."

"An offshore corporation owns the condominium she lives in."

"Yes, I know. My campaign manager arranged it. He funded it through a shell corporation I own, but it was my money. My father and I have done very well in the oil and natural gas business. I thought the condo would be a good investment."

"Did your wife know about the condo?"

"No. I wanted it kept secret. That's why I asked Raymond Finch to arrange its purchase."

"So, your relationship with Ms. Rockwell began as an affair?" I asked.

"Yes."

"And how did you react when you learned Ms. Rockwell was pregnant?"

"I was thrilled. I have no children of my own."

"And your wife? Was she thrilled?"

Trent responded angrily, "I know what you're trying to do. I married Tammy before I went into the Marine Corps. When I came back from the Gulf War, our relationship had changed. I knew she had had an affair with someone in my absence, but I couldn't prove it. Before both of us realized that our relationship had hit a brick wall, I had run for Congress and won. Then the timing for a divorce was horrible. So, we've stayed together to maintain appearances. We've both come to a place where we're ready to move on."

"Then why did you keep Ms. Rockwell and the condo a secret?"

"Affairs don't play well in politics. The press would have roasted me had they found out."

"And now?"

"I'm hoping you'll work with me to keep this out of the press. If you can't, I understand. With my forthrightness about my relationship with Vicky, I hope to show you I had nothing to do with what happened to her."

"Where were you Sunday night?"

"I was in Ponte Verde Beach playing in a pro-am golf event."

Eddy Rand opened a folder and produced receipts. He told me I could keep them.

"Were you aware Vicky's real name was Sally McCoy?" I asked Trent.

"Yes, I was."

"Were you aware of her activities as a prostitute?"

Trent looked at Rand, swallowed hard and said, "Yes. Not at first, but when she found out she was pregnant, she told me."

"Were you aware she was blackmailing men she slept with as a prostitute?"

Eddy Rand interjected, "Let me just stipulate to several things to shorten your inquiry and lessen my client's embarrassment. We're aware of all of Ms. Rockwell's illegal activities. Congressman Trent hired me to extricate her from them. When she became pregnant and disclosed the things she was involved in, she said she wanted out of that life. I was facilitating that."

"And what's your understanding of the extent of her illegal activities?" I directed the question to both of them.

Rand answered, "The only other activity we haven't discussed with you is her involvement in drugs."

"As an officer of the court..."

"You don't need to preach to me, Chief McCain. We don't live in a perfect world."

"Congressman, wasn't that a tremendous gamble for you? If someone found out about her background, you could be the target of blackmail, not to mention a scandal in the press."

"You're right, if I had intended to stay in Congress, which I didn't. I had planned to resign next week. That's until Vicky went missing."

"Let me see if I have this straight. Knowing everything you know about her, the prostitution, the drugs and the extortion, you were willing to give up your career in Congress to marry her?"

"I know it doesn't make sense to you, but I loved her. I almost lost my life in Kuwait during the Gulf War. I spent a month in the hospital from a gunshot wound, undergoing several surgeries to remove bullet fragments. That changed me. Afterwards, I took nothing for granted. When I met Vicky, we clicked. She was beautiful, sexy and funny. I liked the way she made me feel. No woman in my life to that point had made me feel that way. Like I said, I wanted what she had, and she felt the same way."

"Were you aware that she was still blackmailing a man named James Hunt?"

"The concrete guy?" Trent answered.

I nodded.

"That was the last one. Yes, we talked about it. She promised me she would drop it."

"Did she?"

"As far as I know," he said.

"Were you aware she was getting threatening communications from him?"

"No, I was not."

"One final question. Why didn't you call the police when you learned she was missing?"

"I was at the golf tournament I just told you about, staying with friends. I didn't know anything was wrong until I arrived home. I learned she was missing from the newspaper. I tried to call her from the golf tournament, but it went to voicemail. It was not unusual for her not to answer."

"Will your wife confirm what you've told us?"

"I'm sure you understand how delicate all this is, Chief McCain. She's aware of Vicky's existence and that I was involved with her, but she's not aware of the details of Vicky's illegal activities. Telling her about those things would change nothing."

"How did your wife handle the news of your infidelity?"

"As I said, our marriage was over before I ran for Congress. Tammy is well-to-do in her own right; she needs nothing from me and wants nothing from me. She has a boyfriend of her own who, I assume, she loves. She can confirm I told her about Vicky, I was away on the day Vicky was killed and that's all."

Downs said, "Congressman, Vicky was murdered between ten p.m. and midnight. Ponte Verde Beach is only an hour and a half drive from Coronado Beach. Do you have witnesses to confirm your alibi during that time?"

Eddy Rand interjected, "I can confirm he was there. I was with him. We were having drinks in the bar, and there were at least a dozen people with us. I'd be happy to give you their names. Now, we've answered you with honesty and proved to you there was no way Congressman Trent was involved. Can we count on you to keep this out of the press?"

"I can try," I said. "I can't guarantee it, though. It also assumes you've been truthful with us."

"Look, Chief," Trent said. "Vicky's death removes the need for me to resign my seat. The weight of her loss is crushing. I'm not an outwardly emotional person. Inside is another matter. Without her around, I need that job. I need to be busy. If it all comes out, my relationship with her and the things she was involved with, so be it. I'll take my lumps, as they say. If you can keep this part of your investigation under wraps, I'd be most appreciative."

I didn't commit to anything. Nor would it have been proper to do so.

"Those are all of our questions for now," I said. "We may have more in the future."

Eddy Rand said, "Just call me, if you do, and I'll arrange a meeting."

Downs, Cahill and I had been in Rand's office for less than an hour. I suggested we return to my office, and we walked the two long blocks back to the PD.

In my office, Jim Cahill said, "You buying any of that?"

I sat behind the desk, and Cahill and Downs sat in the guest chairs.

I said, "I have to admit, I find it all a little hard to believe. And convenient."

"The guy has an iron-clad alibi," Downs said. "On top of it, he has an attorney for an eyewitness. I'm sure by now, Rand has reduced his testimony to a signed and witnessed affidavit."

"So, you buy into all that junk about him knowing and accepting the prostitution and extortion and still loving her? And after everything Belford told us about McCoy, do you buy into the assumption she felt the same way about Trent?"

"From everything we've learned about McCoy," Downs replied, "she was model-beautiful and could be charming, and she had her sights set on Trent. It is clear to me from all the men she had seduced and blackmailed that she could convince the man she was with that she was totally into him. It doesn't surprise me that Trent felt McCoy loved him. Whether McCoy was capable of loving anyone or not, two of the men she was closest to, Belford and Trent, were both in love with her. What she felt about either of these men, we will never know. As fabricated as his version sounds, I believe him."

"So, you think Trent was an unwitting dupe?"

"I have this picture of an extremely ambitious woman who used her physical assets to capitalize on men's sexual weaknesses. Trent was the ultimate prize. He's attractive, rich, powerful and vulnerable. She convinced him she loved him, and perhaps she conned him. Even after he discovered all the things she was involved in, she still had him wrapped around her finger. McCoy had nothing but her looks and wits, and she parlayed them into a small fortune and a relationship with a man who could fulfill her need for power. Did she love him? Who knows? I doubt it. Is Trent our killer? If he is, his acting deserves an Academy Award, not to mention his airtight alibi."

Cahill said, "Jed, I know you like this guy for it, but I agree with Downs. I want to verify Trent was in Ponte Verde Beach when he said he was, but I think he's telling the truth. I think McCoy was using him, conning him even, but he's convinced she loved him."

"What about his wife?" I asked. "I found his answers regarding her too pat. We've a man, a congressman for that matter—a very public figure—who has been having an affair with a now-pregnant twentysomething. Downs, if you were his wife, how would you react if you knew about the prostitution, extortion and drugs?"

"It would depend on how I felt about him. If what Trent said was true, I might greet all of it as good news. It would assure me incredible advantage in a divorce proceeding. If I loved him and he did that to me, I'd want to kill him or her or both."

"Let's talk with Mrs. Trent," I said.

Cahill stood and said, "If it will help, I'll check out the congressman's alibi while you and Downs talk with Mrs. Trent. I have to be in the office in an hour. I have to run."

Downs said, "You want to interview Mrs. Trent now?"

"Yes," I said, "as soon as you can get an address."

Downs stood. "I'll go work on it."

Downs and Cahill left the office.

I thought about the complexity of this case and the number of people who had the motive to kill Sally McCoy, and yet, we seemed miles away from a viable suspect. I liked Trent for the murder. In New York, I had worked many high-profile cases where men—and women, too—in positions of power operated as though they were above the law. They could be arrogant, hide behind lawyers and use their influence to thwart an investigation. I had suspected that Trent, because of his position, belonged to that ilk. I had been surprised, shocked even, at Trent's openness. Like all the other men Sally McCoy had played, he was vulnerable, searching for elusive happiness—a desperate man. I felt sorry for Trent. His enormous unfulfilled needs made him an easy target. I had pinned my hopes on him as a suspect, but now, I had to admit, we were no closer to finding McCoy's killer than the day we'd found her floating on Disappearing Island.

21

I walked out to Martha Johnson's cubicle.

"What's the latest with your son?"

She spun around in her swivel chair to face me. "There were no prints or any other useful evidence from my house or car. They've canvassed my neighborhood twice, and no one saw anything. My landlord just asked me to leave after she saw what happened to her house. On top of that, it may be months before Deshon has to testify. They're working through a relocation strategy, and whether I'm part of the witness protection effort."

"Maybe you and Deshon should reconsider him testifying."

"If he doesn't testify, they'll try him as an adult. You and I both know prison will destroy him."

"Maybe your attorney can get him off."

"That video of those boys beating the man to death is so damaging, it can't be risked. Besides, all of the boys Deshon was with have been charged and arraigned for manslaughter. As brutal as that beating was, they could all get the maximum sentence of fifteen years. His gang knew an hour after the police picked them up that those prosecutors had peeled Deshon off from the rest of them. It can't be undone, even if we wanted to."

"How is Deshon taking it?"

"He's scared, and he doesn't even know about them coming after me."

"How about you?"

"It's a nightmare, Jed. And all of the options are horrific."

"I'm sorry, Martha."

"It isn't your fault, Chief. It's just the way things go."

"Where are you staying tonight?"

"I won't know until later this afternoon."

"Call me when you find out. If you're staying with Downs, I want to make sure we have a detail there."

Downs texted me that she was in the parking lot and ready to go.

I asked Martha Johnson, "Are you going to be okay?"

"I'm praying for the strength to deal with this one day at a time. That's all I can do."

The Trents had built their home on Quay Assisi, a road lined with multi-million-dollar homes that backed onto wide canals that led to the Indian River. Their home was of Spanish architecture, with soaring gables and lavish tropical landscaping.

Downs had done a quick background check on Tamara Trent and filled me in as we approached their home and turned into the driveway. A Vassar-educated liberal arts major and successful novelist, Tamara Trent engaged in charitable work in the community.

An attractive woman with red hair cut in pageboy fashion answered the door.

We confirmed she was Tamara Trent, introduced ourselves and asked if we could speak with her.

She escorted us to a family room with plate-glass windows and sliding glass doors that overlooked the water. The furnishings were traditional, in beiges and warm colors. A couch and several large padded chairs surrounded a large eight-sided solid oak coffee table. Behind the home, a cabin cruiser with a tall flying bridge rocked in its moorings. Tall outriggers whipped back and forth with the motion of the boat.

Downs and I sat on the couch, Mrs. Trent in a chair, and we declined her offer of something to drink. She wore no makeup; she had pale green eyes and a face filled with freckles. She was slender and graceful in her movements.

"You're here about that woman."

I said, "You may know her as Vicky Rockwell." Downs and I had agreed on our way to the Trents' home that I'd lead the interview.

Mrs. Trent said, "I read in the newspaper that her name was Sally McCoy."

"That's correct. What do you know about her?"

"Only what I read in the paper and what my husband has told me about her, that he had an affair with her, she became pregnant, he was in love with her and wanted a divorce."

"How did you feel about that?"

"I told him he was an idiot for wanting to throw his career away."

"How did you feel about him divorcing you for a younger woman?"

She stared at me for several moments. "You think I had something to do with this?"

"Did you have something to do with this?"

"Let's just cut to the chase. I've never even met the woman, much less killed her. And I've long ago ceased to care what my husband does. My concern is his indiscretions will become a public embarrassment that will affect my career."

"As a writer?"

"Yes."

"Why haven't you and the congressman sought a divorce sooner?" I asked.

"When Bill ran for Congress, his notoriety was helpful to both of us. I had just started writing, and his fame opened doors to publishers I'd have never had access to. There are many financial advantages to holding a congressional seat. He was in no hurry for a divorce, and neither was I."

"Your husband mentioned you were in a relationship of your own."

"That's none of your business."

"Can you account for your whereabouts on Sunday between ten p.m. and five a.m. the next morning?"

"I was with someone. That's also none of your business."

"Mrs. Trent, I see you have a boat, and there are several ways Sally McCoy could have been a threat to you. You have motive, the means to carry out her murder, and, without a proper alibi, you had the opportunity. If you would like to cut to the chase, as you put it, then you can answer my question. Were you involved in a relationship with someone?"

"Yes," she seethed.

"Is this the person you were with on the night of the murder?"

"Yes."

"I'll need a name, please."

"Why do you believe I'd have anything to do with that girl's death? I came into this marriage with more wealth than I know what to do with. When my father passed away several years ago, his wealth combined with mine put my portfolio in the hundreds of millions. I don't need Bill Trent's money. If anything, it is the reverse. His tryst, and the woman's pregnancy, would have been favorable to me in a settlement. She was more helpful to me alive than dead."

"Then you won't mind us confirming your alibi."

"I'm sorry, Chief McCain. I'll not give you his name. I'd ruin this man with a scandal if this became public. You're just fishing at this point, and I won't jeopardize this man's reputation. If you wish to pursue this further, I'd like to have my attorney present, but I can assure you I had nothing to do with that girl's death."

Downs asked, "Do you think your husband is capable of doing this?"

"We were unable to have children. I had a hysterectomy as a young woman. Bill wanted to adopt, but I was unwilling. I just couldn't bring myself to take responsibility for another woman's child. When Bill told me about this girl's pregnancy, he was ecstatic. He was desperate for a child. There's no way he could have killed that girl. No way."

"He told us he was willing to give up his seat in Congress if his relationship with McCoy caused a scandal."

"Again, I think he was desperate enough for a child, he would have given up his seat. No question. He doesn't need the money. With his own fortune, and what he would get in a settlement from my estate, he would have been very comfortable."

I decided not to press confirmation of her alibi for now. If it became an issue, I could always pursue it.

I thanked Mrs. Trent for seeing us, and she showed us to the door.

In the car, I asked Downs for her impression of the interview.

"My impression is the rich are just as screwed up as we are. For all their fancy homes and cars, they're trying to find the same thing we are, to be happy."

"And not succeeding," I said.

Downs started the car and backed out of the driveway. "Are you happy, McCain?"

"What kind of a question is that?"

"An honest one. It deserves an honest answer."

"I'm not unhappy, if that's what you're asking."

"You're dodging my question."

I looked at her as she pulled out onto Quay Assisi. There was a faint smile on her face. "You're enjoying yourself, aren't you?"

"Just answer my question."

"I like my job. Financially, I'm set. I like my house and being on the water. I don't owe any money except for the mortgage on my house."

"Do those things make you happy? The Trents have all of that, but it is obvious they're not happy."

"Downs, you need to get to the point."

"Are you happy being single? Not having a family? Trent was desperate for that."

"Downs, we are not going to have a discussion about this."

"Why not?"

"Because it is inappropriate."

"How?"

"This isn't a discussion about whether I'm happy; this is a discussion of you and me."

"I'm that obvious."

"Yes. Do you believe Mrs. Trent's story?"

"We're changing the subject?"

"Yes."

"She supports her husband's story. While they could have coordinated a response, I don't think they'd have had the time. Why didn't you quiz her about McCoy's extracurricular activities?"

"I guess I didn't want to blow up a man's career. If I shared that information with her, she might have used it in their divorce proceedings, and that could have gone public."

"Men sticking up for men?"

"What purpose would it have served, Downs?"

"None, I guess, for now anyway."

"Exactly."

It was mid-afternoon. I wanted to interview James Hunt and Demarcus Brown. Brown was in Daytona Beach, and I'd have to coordinate with Chief Downs to interrogate him. Since we were out and I had some time before my dinner date with Ashley Rand, I suggested we interview James Hunt. While Trent's version of events with Sally McCoy appeared to track, without a verified alibi for Tamara Trent, I was not willing to rule her out. Until Cahill verified Trent's presence in the bar at the time of the murder, he was still on my list too.

22

James Hunt's office was in a different building at Southeast Volusia Materials than the concrete plant and dispatch office where I'd met Patrick McCoy. Downs parked at the headquarters building, and we badged the receptionist. She asked for our names and called to announce to someone that we were there to see Mr. Hunt.

An older woman dressed in a dark pantsuit escorted us down a long hall to French doors marked with a sign that read Executive Offices.

Inside, the woman asked us to sit in a waiting area, and she disappeared into an office.

After a few moments, a man in his mid-fifties, about six feet tall and two hundred pounds, appeared in the waiting area. He had short brown hair, and his stomach hung over his belt.

"I'm James Hunt." He extended his hand to me. "And you are?"

I shook his hand. "Chief McCain with the Coronado Beach Police Department, and this is Lieutenant Leslie Downs."

Hunt then shook Downs' hand. "What's this regarding?"

I said, "Could we discuss this somewhere with more privacy."

"Yes, of course."

Hunt led us a short distance down another hall into a large office with a plate-glass window that overlooked a huge quarry, where excavators were digging in a pit and mammoth dump trucks were hauling material to unknown destinations. Hunt's overpowering solid walnut desk and chairs were positioned against the opposite wall to the window to give the occupant a view sitting at the desk. There was a long conference table with a dozen chairs around it, and then a low couch and several chairs in a cluster. He showed us to his desk, which he sat behind, and we occupied the chairs in front of him. I couldn't be certain whether he'd designed it that way, but his chair behind the desk was higher than the chairs we were sitting in. It gave you the impression he was looking down at you.

"Now, what's this about?" he asked.

"Do you know a woman by the name of Vicky Rockwell?" Downs asked.

"No, that name doesn't sound familiar to me."

"She's the woman blackmailing you."

"I told you, I don't know what you're talking about."

"It's the woman you paid more than eighty thousand dollars to."

"I still have no idea what you're talking about."

"We have video of you and Ms. Rockwell engaged in sex. We have your fingerprints all over the house where they videotaped you. We have copies of the emails between you and Ms. Rockwell about the blackmail. I can get a warrant to examine all your financial transactions to prove you paid her for the first installment. Now do you still want to deny you know Ms. Rockwell?"

Hunt dropped his head so his chin rested on his chest. "All right! I knew her."

"Tell us how you met her."

"At a fundraiser for Congressman Trent. She introduced herself to me and told me how thrilled she was to meet me. She was beautiful, and she wore a skimpy cocktail dress that was cut very low in the front."

"You didn't find this odd at a fundraiser?"

"I had already had several scotches. Nothing seemed odd."

"Were there drugs at this party?"

"Yes. It was done on the lowdown, but yes."

"Were you partaking?"

"No."

"What happened next?"

"She stayed with me most of the night, flirting and talking. I assumed her purpose was to show me a good time, so I'd make a large contribution. I was a supporter of Trent and had made large contributions in the past. As the evening wound down, she told me she wanted to see me again. And she made it clear our relationship would progress to the next level."

I asked, "The sexual level?"

"Yes. She handed me her business card and said to get in touch via the email address on the card."

"And when did you do that?" Downs asked.

"About three months ago. She invited me for drinks at her house at Bethune Beach."

"What happened next?"

"A month later, I get an email from her threatening to expose me. I responded that she could go screw herself. Then I received pictures in the mail she threatened to send to my wife and the newspaper. The note with it said I was to put eighty thousand in cash in a locker at the bowling alley by a certain date and time."

"And you paid it?"

"Yes. And two weeks later, she demanded another eighty grand."

"Is that when you threatened her? When you told her if you found her, you would kill her?"

"I didn't threaten her."

Downs said, "I have the email, Mr. Hunt. I remember it word for word."

"All right, yes, I threatened her."

"What happened then?" I asked.

"She raised the blackmail amount to one hundred thousand. I had no choice; I told my wife. I wasn't about to give that bitch another dime."

"Did you have any more contact with her?"

"No. The next I heard, she was dead."

"Were you aware Vicky Rockwell's name was Sally McCoy?"

"No."

"Did you know Patrick McCoy, an employee of yours, was her father?"

"No, I didn't know. McCoy has worked for me for years. Good man. She was his daughter? I remember, and this was a long way back, he was having problems with his daughter. I can't remember what it was about, but he missed quite of bit of time at work as a result. I remember a scrawny little girl they brought to company cookouts, but that was years ago."

"Mr. Hunt, how did your wife react to the news of your affair with Rockwell?" I asked.

"She was furious. She was pissed I had given any money to the woman."

"Do you own a boat?"

"Yes, a fishing boat."

"Where do you moor it?" I asked.

"I rent a slip at the Coronado Marina."

"Where were you on Sunday night between ten p.m. and five the next morning?"

"I was in Atlanta at a business meeting."

"Can you prove you were there?"

"Yes. I fill out an expense report after all my trips. My receipts will prove it."

"We would like a copy, please, before we leave."

"Did your wife travel with you?" Downs asked.

"No. She seldom does."

"Those are all the questions we have for now." I pulled a card from my wallet and handed it to him. "If you think of anything that could be helpful, please call."

Hunt left his office for several minutes and returned with copies of his expense report. I leafed through it, found that he'd driven, stayed at the Marriot Marquis in downtown Atlanta and had a meal in the hotel restaurant at nine p.m., and it would have been impossible for him to be in Coronado Beach on the night of Sally McCoy's death.

When we left the office, I told Downs, "I want a search warrant of the Hunt home and their boat. We're looking for any signs of cyanide at the home and any trace evidence that they could have transported McCoy on their boat. Also, I want a warrant for Hunt's email provider. I want copies of all the emails for Hunt's account."

"We have copies of what McCoy left on her computer. I guess it won't hurt to make sure there aren't more emails between them."

We jumped into the car. On the way back to the PD, Downs asked, "What're you thinking?"

"I don't know, Downs. I don't feel comfortable with the connection between Hunt and Patrick McCoy. That's too much of a coincidence."

"All right. When we get to the PD, I'll work on the warrants. When do you want to serve them?"

"I want to talk to Demarcus Brown first thing in the morning, but I have to coordinate with your father. I'd like to talk to Brown while you're serving the warrants. Once we've searched the Hunt home, I want to talk to Mrs. Hunt."

"I'll call my father and work out a meeting with Brown. Are you thinking Mrs. Hunt is the killer?"

"I have no idea. We haven't talked to her, but she has motive and means."

"We're running out of suspects, McCain."

"Whoever killed Sally McCoy is right under our nose, Downs."

"What about Demarcus Brown?"

"I could be wrong," I said, "but I don't see Brown as a suspect. Perhaps after I talk to him, I'll feel different, but there was nothing going down between them that would provide Brown an incentive to kill her."

"What about the drug transaction ledger? If Brown knew about it, wouldn't that be motive?"

"Sure, but you found it in her safe. If she planned to use it against Brown, it would have either been in the possession of law enforcement, or there would have been some evidence in her computer or on her phone that she was using it against him."

Downs said, "Anyone who went through the trouble to keep such a detailed account of their transactions with Brown wanted more than just an insurance policy if they were caught. Something is going on there, McCain. Maybe I missed something."

"Do you want me to postpone questioning Brown?"

"No. I've no plans tonight. I'll go back through her texts and emails again. Call me on your way to Daytona, and I'll let you know if I've found anything."

23

On the way home, after Downs had called her father, Chief Downs called me.

"I'll pick up Brown, and we'll bring him in for questioning, but you can't talk about the ledger you found."

"Why not?"

"We talked about this. Brown is a small fish in a larger pond. I want to take down the whole organization. We've lost seventeen people to drug overdoses this month alone, four of them minors. The heroin and crack epidemics are worse than I've ever seen. I want Brown and the whole organization."

"Can't you use the ledger to flip Brown?"

"Yes, and I know who Brown buys from, but I don't know how big the organization is above him. With the ledger, I can pull Brown in anytime I want. But the steps after are unclear."

"What about the joint task force?"

"They hear rumors of who the players are, but we've nothing concrete. For now, I don't want to tip my hand."

"So, I have no leverage to use in questioning him."

"No, not now. Do you still want to talk with him?"

"Yes."

"All right, I'll pick him up. What time?"

"Nine in the morning."

"You mind if I sit in?"

"Your turf. Absolutely not."

I pulled in the drive to my home. The house looked worn and dated. I had cleaned up the yard and repaired the sprinkler system. What St. Augustine grass there was had overtaken the weeds to produce what passed for a lawn. It was a beginning. The challenge of transforming this structure into something the neighbors wouldn't complain about seemed daunting.

I showered, dressed, pulled a beer from the refrigerator and walked out to the dock. The sun was low in the sky, I could hear thunder off to the west, there was a strong breeze coming out of the east and the humidity was oppressive.

When I twisted the top off the bottle, I could hear footsteps behind me and turned to see AJ.

"Just the man I was looking for," AJ said, sitting down on the bench beside me.

"What in the hell did you do?"

"I quit." He looked at my beer and asked, "You have another one of those?"

I stood up, walked to the kitchen, pulled another beer out of the refrigerator and walked back out.

"Here," I said as I twisted off the cap and handed him the sweating brown bottle.

He raised his beer bottle and clicked it against mine. "To better days."

I sat down. "Why did you quit?"

"Jed, I'm an old man. I've had my chance in the sun. When they arrested Mayor Parker, the city needed someone to step into the job to stabilize things. I did that."

"The city still needs you, AJ You shocked Neil Jarret."

"I'd have loved to have seen the expression on his face when he received my email."

"You didn't talk to him about this?"

"He didn't come to see me when he fired you. He didn't come to me to tell me my relationship with you was causing him problems."

"You have a pretty good relationship with him, don't you?"

"Yeah, I did. What he did to you was shitty. He could have worked it out. He chose not to."

"He needs you, AJ."

"The city needs a good chief of police more than they need me. I thought my solution was a good one."

"Good for me, but not for you. Bad for Jarret, too. I know he was counting on your support to push through improvements he wants to make in the city. There has to be some other way to solve this. It was clear from my discussion with Jarret that he hadn't expected your resignation. Maybe it will be enough to loosen him up a little."

"He's right about one thing, Jed. I'm not impartial. This town needs you. The police department needs you. Grizzle resisted changes to modernize the department. You've done more in six months than he did in his entire tenure with us. I'll not be the reason for your firing."

"Will you stay in the job if I resign?"

"That won't happen."

"Will you stay if I can work something out with Jarret?"

"I'm doubtful that's possible, but I'll reserve judgment until you have something. Until then, my resignation stands. My relationship with you and your future are more important to me than an ill-paying part-time job."

I didn't say anything and took a swig of my beer.

He said, "So, when are you going to do something with this piece-of-shit house of yours? If you just painted this place, the value of my house would go up thirty grand." He tipped up his bottle, finishing off the beer. "Looks like a crack house." He winked.

"You're relentless."

AJ stood, patted me on the shoulder, left the dock and walked across his manicured yard to his meticulously maintained home.

24

I had agreed to pick Ashley Rand up at her home on Riverside Drive. She'd told me where she lived and described it to me over the phone, so I knew which house it was. An Art Deco style, it looked like something Frank Lloyd Wright would have designed in the 1950s. Riverside Drive followed the bank of the Indian River. Elegant homes with riparian rights to the water faced the waterway. Whenever I had to go to the south side of the city or to the Edgewater PD, I drove by her home and admired it.

Rand was sitting on her front porch waiting on me when I arrived. When I pulled into her driveway, she stood, stepped down off the porch and strolled toward my truck. She had her long black hair in a single braid that hung over her right shoulder. Her sleeveless orange V-neck T-shirt dress hugged her body like a second skin, the hem catching her mid-thigh. She wore spaghetti strap white sandals and held a clutch just large enough for a wallet and keys. She looked stunning. Before I could get out of the truck to walk around and open the door, she was on the passenger side, opened the door and hiked herself up into the truck.

Once in, she tugged at her short skirt, opened the console between our seats and deposited her purse. Her makeup was effective, but spare, and she wore no jewelry. She didn't need them.

I blurted out, "You're...beautiful!"

She smiled. "Don't act so shocked."

"You are."

"Thank you." I could tell my honesty had made her uncomfortable. She changed the subject. "Where are you taking me?"

"I was thinking about Clancy's on Flagler."

"Perfect. I love their food."

"I've never been. AJ has been after me since I arrived here to try it."

"Tonight's the night."

I found a place to park on Flagler Avenue and walked around the truck to open Rand's door, but she'd already slid off the seat to the ground and closed the door.

We were two blocks from the ocean, and the breeze off the water was brisk and refreshing. The sun was setting and painted the high cirrus clouds in pinks and purples. It occurred to me that Coronado Beach had two downtown areas, one on the mainland near the PD on Canal Street and one here on beachside along Flagler Avenue.

"Ashley, how did the city end up with two business districts?" I asked.

"You need a little history lesson, Chief McCain."

As we walked toward the entrance to the restaurant, Rand stood a head shorter than I did. It was a little awkward. I didn't know whether to hold her hand, put my arm around her or walk closer to her. She reached out, took my hand and gave it a squeeze.

The host showed us to our counter-height table by a window looking out on Flagler Avenue. The server, a large woman in her fifties, took our drink order. The room was dark, with a bar in the back. Surfboards of every description hung from the rafters of the open-beamed ceiling.

Rand flipped her braid over her shoulder, put her elbows on the table and folded her hands in front of her.

"Tell me the history, Ashley."

"Coronado Beach used to be two cities, New Smyrna and Coronado Beach. New Smyrna was on the mainland and Coronado Beach on beachside, both with their own city centers. In the 1930s, New Smyrna had water. Coronado Beach didn't. Coronado sits on a sandbar that extends from Ponce Inlet to the end of Canaveral National Seashore and has no access to fresh water. People on the beach used to collect water off their roofs into cisterns. That worked well when it rained, not so well when there wasn't. Coronado had one thing going for it: tax revenue. The oceanfront and waterfront properties produced a disproportionate amount of real estate tax revenue, and beachside property owners controlled the wealth. One city had water, and the other had money. And you know what they say, 'He who has the gold rules.' In the thirties, the two towns merged into Coronado Beach."

I saw, "It seems to me the city has two different cultures and lifestyles."

"The Indian River divides the city in two, and not just geographically. The cultural division is expressed in many different ways."

"When I first came over the South Causeway Bridge and saw the island from the top, I knew this was where I wanted to live. There are many waterways in this town."

"Where do you live?"

"Bouchelle Island. If I threw a rock from my dock over the South Causeway Bridge, I could hit the dock in front of your place."

"It has been a while since I've been on that island. There are some nice homes in there."

"And then there's mine. It needs a lot of work. At least that's what my neighbors keep telling me."

"So, how did you end up in Coronado Beach?"

Our server brought margaritas. We said we wanted to wait before ordering our meals.

I gave Rand the short version. When I'd retired, I'd wanted a second retirement in Florida, and Sarah James had found me this job. I told her the weird circumstances of how it had evolved into the chief's position.

She said, "Grizzle was a piece of work."

"That's the kindest way to put it. I'm learning he was not well liked."

"That's good for you, Jed. It means people in the community will have low expectations."

"Did you hear AJ McFarland quit?"

"Yes. Did it have anything to do with your situation?"

"He thought it would save my job. I don't think the city manager was expecting that to happen. He's in a bit of a panic."

"Does this help or hurt you?"

"I don't know. Whichever way this goes, someone is going to get hurt."

"How?"

"AJ is alone. His wife passed away a year ago, and he has poured himself into the welfare of this city. He needs his job. Without it, he would lose purpose. He derives great pleasure from serving others, and I'll not be the reason he gives that up. The city manager will lose a strong advocate who has repeatedly rallied support for Jarret's agenda."

"And how will you lose?"

"When I came, I had no thought of ever being chief. My goal was to be a detective, put in another twenty years and then retire. The chief job was dropped into my lap when Grizzle quit. When Sarah James was killed, it made me regret having accepted the job. Over the past six months, I've been trying to make up my mind if I want to remain in that position. When Jarret fired me, it made me realize how much I like what I am doing. I'm having a hard time finding a way where everyone can win—where AJ stays, I stay, and Jarret is comfortable."

"Tell me about Sarah James."

I told Rand that Sarah was my boss with the NYPD, about the Night Fire Strangler being her ex-fiancé, and how he'd cost Sarah her career with the department. I explained Sarah's desire to have a relationship with me, that my divorce from my wife had stood in the way, and how guilty I had felt upon her death that I hadn't pursued her sooner.

"You were in love with her."

"Yes."

"You have regrets?"

"They are legion."

"Tell me about them."

"Do you want to hear this?"

Our server came and took our order for another round of drinks.

"Yes," Rand said.

"I failed to protect her from that monster, and she lost her life because of me. I don't think I'll ever get past that. My main regret? Sarah expressed her love for me, and for a variety of reasons, I failed to act on it. At first, it was because I was married to a woman who was cheating on me. Then it was out of some sense of loyalty to the department since Sarah and I worked together, and then they forced Sarah out. Next, it was the distance between us. She took a job in Tallahassee, and I was still in New York until I retired. It wasn't until I moved here that I let myself act on the feelings I had for her. I missed so much. Then she was gone."

"How old are you, Jed?"

"I just turned forty-two two weeks ago."

"I'm thirty-six, and I have regrets, too. The greatest of them is I married a man who in the end found a man more attractive than me. I regret that I spent fifteen years of my life trying to build something with Eddy only to find out he didn't love me. I don't think I could handle that kind of rejection again."

Our server delivered our second round of drinks. I looked at Ashley Rand and thought she was the most desirable woman I had ever met. Sarah James had been beautiful, but Rand smoldered in ways I didn't understand. Her dress was revealing, and she was blessed physically, but the heat I felt was coming from something deeper. While the sexual attraction was mutual, I recognized she was still tender from the rejection of her husband. She was putting herself out there, and I needed to handle her feelings with great care. *I don't think I could handle that kind of rejection again* hung in the air like a warning shot across my bow.

"I'll have to remember that for future reference," I said, quoting her from the day before. What I wanted to say was *You're one of the most desirable women I've ever met*, but I didn't. I knew if I said it, I'd cross a line we might not be ready to cross. "We're both still healing, Ashley."

"I'm attracted to you, and I feel comfortable when I'm with you."

She had told me this before.

She continued, "As an attorney, I get involved in the aftermath of failed relationships. What seems good at first can fall away. Are you willing to take it slow?"

"I'm looking forward to it."

When I spoke those words to her, I knew, from the chemistry I felt with her, that things—even with our best efforts—would not move slowly.

25

Downs called me at two o'clock in the morning. "I didn't think you were going to answer your phone."

"It's the middle of the night, Downs. What time is it?"

She didn't answer my question. "I'm at Halifax Medical Center's ER. Deshon Johnson has been shot. He's in surgery. I'm with Martha Johnson here at the hospital, but she's inconsolable."

"What happened?"

"The gang found the location of the safe house. They busted through the front door and used automatic weapons on the two cops guarding Deshon. One of the officers returned fire and killed one of the gang members, but not before two others put three slugs in Deshon. The officer who returned fire radioed for help and an ambulance before he bled out. When they found Deshon, he was still breathing."

"How many of them were there?"

"When the officer called in, he said there were four men."

"Both cops are dead?"

"Yes. They both died at the scene. You should come down. Martha blames herself for all of this, and I can't calm her down."

I used lights and siren, but it still took twenty minutes to reach the hospital. I parked, ran into the ER and was directed to the surgical waiting area. Even before the elevator door opened, I could hear the wailing of Martha Johnson. I ran toward her cries and walked into the waiting area, where a doctor, still in surgical garb, tried in vain to comfort her.

"Oh, God, I can't believe this," Johnson kept repeating. The surgeon was trying to put his arm around her, but she wouldn't have it.

I moved closer, and, when she noticed me next to her, she threw her arms around me and began to sob, her shoulders heaving. She wailed, "Those monsters killed my boy. Those monsters killed my boy. God, I should never have..." and more uncontrolled crying. She clamped onto me and let her weight fall against me.

"Oh, Martha. I'm sorry." I repeated it several times, for I had no idea what to say to comfort her.

I looked at the surgeon and Downs, shaken by the scene. The surgeon said how sorry he was, patted Martha on the back and began to leave.

"I want to see my boy." The words hissed from her lips.

"Give me a few minutes, and I'll arrange it. I'll call you on the phone in the waiting area." The surgeon pointed to a wall phone near the entrance.

As the surgeon was leaving, Chief Roger Downs stepped out of his way and entered the room, searching for clues as to what had happened. Without us speaking to him, I saw recognition wipe across his face. His expression spoke of his own profound loss.

When Martha recognized Chief Downs, she flew into a rage. "You bastard. You bastard!" She tried to pull away from me. "You were supposed to protect my boy. You said he would be safe. You got him killed. He didn't stand a chance."

Wisely, the chief didn't try to defend himself. He said, "I failed, and I've lost two very good men and your son as a result. I can't begin to express my deep sorrow,

Martha." Chief Downs broke into tears. He pulled his arms around his chest as if trying to hug himself. Martha broke away from me and fell into Chief Downs' chest. He put his arms around her, and they cried together. They remained in an embrace until the wall phone rang. I answered. It was the surgeon directing us to the recovery room.

The scene in Recovery was heart-rending. Chief Downs held Martha Johnson until she asked the attending nurse if she could hold her boy. She approached her son as though she were appraising him. She scooped him up by passing an arm under his neck, and she pulled him into an embrace. "I'm sorry, Deshon." She held him and cried for several minutes, and then she laid him down again and brushed his forehead as a mother might comfort a child with a fever. She watched her son for a few moments, tried to compose herself, then picked up the sheet and covered his head. She backed away from the bed and said, "Thank you," to the nurse.

I asked Chief Downs to step out into the hallway.

Before I could say anything to him, he said, "It used to be people held the police in high regard, and if they didn't, they at least feared us. Today, it is open season on cops. It's a war where the enemy is better armed and has the press and court system on their side. You know what, McCain? The days of me trying to walk a fine line of political correctness are over, and I don't give a shit what the consequences will be. I don't care what I have to do. I'm going after those motherfuckers until every one of them is behind bars or dead, and I don't care which."

I tried to say something to support him, but he spoke again before I had the chance.

"Before I came here, I had to console the two families of the men I lost tonight. I hate this part of this job. I'll not rest until these bastards are dead or in jail, McCain. I can't make that promise to Johnson, but I'm telling you. I have to go. The press will have a field day with this, and I need to do damage control. I'll give Martha a day or two and look in on her. Tough day, McCain."

I said, "They don't get any tougher."

As I turned to head back to join Downs and Martha Johnson, they were coming out of Recovery. Martha was still emotional but more in control. Downs had her arm around her and gave me a helpless look that said, *Where do we go from here?*

"What would you like to do?" I asked Martha.

"What I want to do and what I should do are two different things." She dabbed her eyes with tissue. "What I want to do is get my gun and hunt down every one of those..." She wiped her eyes again. "I should have never let my boy testify. This is my fault. When they firebombed my car, I knew they wouldn't stop. When they destroyed my house, I should have pulled Deshon out of protective custody and left town. I knew better."

"You can't blame yourself, Martha," I said, knowing it seemed hollow, but I had to react to her ill logic. I wanted to tell her she'd done the right thing, but no amount of evidence would convince her. I said instead, "You had no idea they'd do something like this. Every reasonable precaution was taken."

"Well, it wasn't enough, and now my son is dead. I'll never forgive myself."

We three stood in the hallway, still unsure where to go or what to do until Martha said, "I don't want to leave Deshon." She retraced her steps, and Downs and I followed her back to the surgical waiting area, went inside and sat in one of the chairs lined up against the wall.

"Would you like me to stay with you?" I asked.

"Please. If it wouldn't be too much trouble."

I said to Downs, "Leslie, why don't you go home and try to get some sleep."

"What about you?"

"I have to be in Daytona in the morning to interview Demarcus Brown," I said.

"Will you talk with me in the hall, please?" When I followed her into the hall, she asked, "How will you get Martha back to my place?"

"I don't know. She doesn't feel comfortable leaving. I'm following her lead."

Downs said, "I can come back and pick her up if needed. Just call me. When Martha called me earlier, I was just going back through Sally McCoy's emails and text messages. I was looking for anything that might tie Brown to her murder, and I did find something. I also found interesting emails she sent to her father and to James Hunt. I obtained the warrant to search Hunt's email account. I should have brought them with me, but when my dad called me about Deshon, I dropped everything to drive Martha here. You should review them before you interview Brown."

"Can you give me the short version?"

"She was blackmailing Brown. And she was trying to destroy her father."

"Go home. Either I'll bring Martha by your house later, or you can pick her up here. I'll get the file from you then."

Downs left, and I went back into the waiting area and sat down beside Johnson. Her crying was soft. I asked her if I could get her anything. She said she just wanted to sit with me. I had no words of consolation and didn't offer any.

We sat in silence until five-thirty in the morning. Then she stood up and said she wanted to go to Lesley Downs' home.

I called Chief Downs and asked if he could have one of his officers drive us to Coronado Beach. When the unmarked car arrived, I texted Downs and warned her of our arrival. When we pulled into her drive, she was waiting on the porch, holding a file. She walked to the passenger side, intercepted Johnson and handed the file to me.

I got out and circled the car while Downs gave Johnson a hug. Then Downs put her arms around me and hugged me fiercely, and I could tell she was struggling to keep her composure. I returned her embrace. I thought, with my focus on Johnson, I had overlooked the emotional damage Downs had sustained that night. Downs pulled away and put an arm around Johnson, and they walked onto her porch and then into the house.

26

I drove home, showered, changed clothes, made some coffee and sat on the dock, going through the file Downs had given me. Downs had divided the material between those pertaining to Brown and those related to Sally McCoy and her father.

From the emails to Brown, it was clear she had been shaking him down, threatening to go to the police with the ledger. Downs had copies of McCoy's emails to Brown, but nothing from him. There was no indication he'd acknowledged her extortion. Downs' notes in the margins said she hadn't found evidence in McCoy's financial records or electronics that Brown had ever paid her. The emails were recent, the latest sent a week before someone had killed McCoy.

The other packet showed emails to both James Hunt and McCoy's father. McCoy's email to Hunt acknowledged he hadn't paid her the second installment of a hundred thousand dollars she'd demanded, and McCoy had offered an alternative method of payment. She said if Hunt fired Patrick McCoy, she would consider his debt paid, and she would destroy the evidence of their involvement.

The email to her father was one sentence. "You'll pay for what you did to me."

The Brown emails plainly showed he had motive to kill Sally McCoy. This created a conflict with Roger Downs. Chief Downs had agreed to pull Brown in for questioning provided I didn't divulge the existence of the ledger. The ledger, however, may have been the motive for killing her. Chief Downs and I needed to resolve this issue before my interview with Brown.

The Patrick McCoy angle explained the connection between Hunt and Patrick. Sally had been using Hunt to get to her father. Why? It was obvious, since Patrick McCoy had still been working at the concrete plant when I'd interviewed him, that Hunt hadn't fired him, or if he had, it hadn't taken effect yet. Since there was no email response from either man, I had no way of knowing whether Hunt had fired Patrick McCoy.

I emailed Downs to find out how Johnson was doing. She texted back that Johnson had collapsed from exhaustion and was sleeping. Downs said she would stay with her and work from home. I asked her if there was any other correspondence between McCoy and her father. She said I had everything she had.

I called Chief Downs about the evidence that McCoy had blackmailed Brown and that a potential murder charge trumped his racketeering investigation. Chief Downs was adamant I couldn't interview Brown unless I agreed not to mention the ledger.

"What if he brings it up? What if he volunteers it?"

"Chief McCain, I know this investigation is important to you, but I've lost two officers, and I have kids dropping like flies from the shit this dirtbag is pumping out. I have an opportunity to clean up the streets, and I have every intention of succeeding. You confirm to him we have that ledger, and he'll go underground. I'm over going to funerals. Are we clear?"

I told him I was. Without the ability to mention the ledger, I couldn't mention the blackmail.

Demarcus Brown was an enormous man. At least three hundred pounds. His puffed-up face resembled an overstuffed cabbage patch doll. He wore his hair in dreadlocks that hung to his hunched shoulders. He wore a tent-size orange tank top, and every finger on both hands was adorned with a ring. He wore what appeared to be large diamond earrings and had a gold stud piercing his lower lip.

Next to Brown was another Black man dressed in a suit. He introduced himself as Cedrick Holmes. He was Brown's attorney.

"I'm Chief McCain with the Coronado Beach Police Department. I'm investigating the death of Sally McCoy," I said to Brown, "but you'll know her by the name Vicky Rockwell."

"Never heard of her." He tried to lean back in the chair with difficulty.

"She was distributing drugs you supplied at parties in the area."

"I told you. Never heard of her." Brown rolled his eyes and stuck a finger in his mouth as though picking his teeth.

"I can produce phone records and text messages that prove she was in communication with you." I knew this was a non-starter since all the calls were to pre-paid phones.

Holmes leaned forward and said, "My client has already told you he doesn't know this woman."

Brown said, "I don't own a cellphone." More eye rolling and fidgeting in the chair, which creaked under his weight.

Without the ledger, I had nothing.

"You thinking I killed this Rockwell girl?"

Holmes interjected, "Mr. Brown, we discussed this."

"You had motive," I said.

"Is this 'bout that woman in the newspaper who was poisoned?"

"So, you did know her?"

"Hell, no. I didn't know her. If I did know her, which I don't, I sure as hell wouldn't have poisoned the bitch."

Holmes said, "That's enough, Mr. Brown. Not another word."

"Why not?" I asked Brown.

"What kind of a pussy do you think I am? Now, like I said, I never heard of the bitch. If I were going to kill someone, I sure as hell wouldn't poison them, man."

Holmes said, "Another word, Mr. Brown, and I'll walk out of here."

"Just saying."

It was clear from Holmes that the interview was over, and since I couldn't produce evidence of the ledger, going any further was futile.

The truth was that as innocuous as the interview was, Brown, for whatever reason, had made a good point. Considering the way the gang had dealt with Deshon Johnson's betrayal, had I been Brown, and had McCoy blackmailed me, I'd have found a more violent means to dispose of her. I would want to send a clear message to others who might have similar ambitions. Poison would be a cowardly way to dispose of an enemy in the world of Demarcus Brown. For me to accuse him of poisoning someone was an affront to his pride. That was the point he'd made.

With Leslie Downs working from home, I called her to confirm she'd obtained a warrant to search Hunt's home and boat. She said she had. She asked me if I wanted her to work on the warrants with me. She said she had Alicia Torres standing by. I told her to have Torres meet me at the PD in thirty minutes. While Torres and I served the warrant on Hunt's home, Torres could have her crew search for trace evidence on the Hunt boat in the marina.

27

The Hunt home was in the Samsula area, west of Coronado Beach. The sign at the entrance read Triple H Ranch. I pointed the cruiser down the shell-based driveway, which led to a large home of modest design. The house was fenced off to prevent nearby cattle from grazing on the manicured yard.

A heavyset blond woman in her fifties with blue eyes answered the door, wearing jeans, a Western shirt and boots; from the way she was perspiring, she'd been working outside.

"I'm Chief Jed McCain from the Coronado Beach Police, and this is Agent Alicia Torres with the FDLE. I have a warrant to search your home." I handed her the search warrant.

She backed away from the door and let us into the house. I noticed just below the house number a small sign read Michelle Hunt, DVM.

"I don't know what you hope to find," she said. "Is this about the Rockwell woman?"

"Yes, ma'am."

"You're not going to find anything. My husband had nothing to do with her death."

"Let us conduct our search, and then we'll talk."

Torres and I had already agreed that what we were looking for was cyanide or anything else that tied the Hunts to the murder.

I said to Torres, "You take the east side of the house. I'll take the other."

I started with the master bedroom bath, checking the medicine cabinets and cabinets below the sinks. Next, I inspected the master closet and the chest of drawers in the bedroom. Down the hall was a bedroom that had been converted into an office. There were several file cabinets, a diploma from the University of Florida School of Veterinarian Medicine hanging on the wall, and a large desk with an L-return. The top of the desk was clean, and the computer on the desk was turned off. The file cabinets were locked. I walked into the hall and called for Dr. Hunt. She followed me into the office.

"Would you open these cabinets, please? And is your desk locked?"

"The file cabinets contain patient files, and the desk has financial information that's personal."

"I have a valid warrant, Dr. Hunt. It'll take just take a moment to confirm what you're telling me."

She made no effort to hide her anger as she unlocked the cabinets and the desk. There was nothing incriminating.

I asked her to turn on her computer and log into her email. She started to object, and I reminded her that the warrant called out email accounts. She complied. I scanned the emails from the last three weeks, and except for junk mail, they were all related to her veterinary practice.

I searched the kitchen and pantry and found nothing suspicious. Downs met me in the living room and shook her head, indicating she hadn't found anything.

"Do you have a clinic here on the property, Dr. Hunt?" I asked.

"It's in the barn. I specialize in horses and cattle."

She led us through the back door and through a fence to a large metal building.

Small fenced-in pens surrounded the building, and the interior had six stalls, all of which were empty. The structure had large sliding doors at each end of the building that permitted a truck and trailer to drive through and unload animals. At the closest end of the building, there was an air-conditioned clinic. In it were cabinets containing medication and surgical supplies, a stainless-steel operating table, two stainless-steel worktables, a hoist to lift animals and a separate small reception area. I asked Torres to check the medications and chemicals. It took us a half-hour to comb through the clinic, without finding anything untoward.

Dr. Hunt led us back to the house, through the back door and into the eat-in kitchen.

She offered us coffee, which we accepted black. "So, did you find what you were looking for?"

We all sat at the kitchen table.

I didn't answer her question. Instead, I asked, "Are you aware Vicky Rockwell was blackmailing your husband?"

"I am."

"And what was your understanding of their relationship?"

Hunt swept her blond hair to the side and curled it over her ear. "That she was a prostitute and took pictures of my husband in her bed."

"When did he tell you about it?" I asked.

"He didn't. I was looking for the telephone number for one of our friends on his cellphone and found an email from that woman. Well, I found several from her."

"Were you aware he'd paid her eighty thousand dollars?"

"Yes."

"He told us he told you after he'd paid her eighty grand, and she tried again to extort him for one hundred thousand."

"He's mistaken. If I hadn't found out about it, the dumb shit would have paid her."

"How did you handle receiving that news?"

"Chief McCain, I'm not stupid. Why don't you ask me if I killed that woman?"

"Did you?"

"No."

"You would agree you had sufficient reason to want her dead?"

"If anything, I'd want my husband dead, but that's another conversation."

"Rockwell was out to ruin your husband."

"At first, we were convinced of that. When we refused to pay a second time, she demanded we fire Pat McCoy. Pat has been with my husband's company for many years."

"So, what did you do?"

"When she demanded an additional one hundred thousand dollars, we told her we wouldn't pay it. We told her if she wanted to go to the police or release the pictures to the newspaper to go ahead. When she demanded we fire McCoy, we did nothing. We never heard from her again. Then we learned she'd been killed."

"Can anyone substantiate you were home on Sunday night?"

"Jim was out of town. I was alone. Here, asleep." She asked me, "Are you single, Chief?"

I nodded.

"On that night, can you prove you were home?"

I chuckled to myself. "Ms. Rockwell was found on Disappearing Island, which can only be reached by boat. Dr. Hunt, you and your husband own a boat. The girl died from cyanide poisoning. You're familiar with cyanide and its chemical composition, and you have the means to create it in your clinic. Your husband cheated on you, and because of this woman, he squandered eighty thousand dollars of your money. You have motive, the means to have committed the crime and the opportunity."

Her face grew redder as I explained my logic. With great effort to restrain her anger, she said, "While I'm angry this woman has stolen so much from us, SHE isn't the one I blame. The blame falls on my husband's shoulders. HE is the one at fault. Because HE couldn't keep it in his pants, HE alone brought all this down on us. And he'll pay for his indiscretion when I finish with divorce proceedings. Every penny that selfish bastard paid that woman will come out of his side of our settlement. If anything, I owe Ms. Rockwell, or whatever the hell her name is, a debt. She exposed my husband for what he is. So, you're wrong about the motive."

"Dr. Hunt, we're executing a search warrant on your boat as we speak. If we find anything that would contradict your story..."

"I was on that boat once three years ago. I don't know what you'll find."

"Would your husband be capable of retaliating against Rockwell?"

"If you'd asked me several months ago, I'd have said there was no way my husband could have done this. Now I have no idea what he's capable of."

28

Torres and I left the Three H Ranch and followed the main highway to town and the Coronado Beach Marina.

"Can we talk about the crime lab?"

"That's what cost me my job, Torres. You can talk, but it won't do any good."

"Hear me out, please."

I looked over at her, her eagerness written in her green eyes. "Okay."

"I put a study together that shows if Coronado Beach would open a crime lab, it would not only pay for itself, but it would also save the city money."

"I'm listening."

"With Cahill's permission, I went back and looked at the money we've charged your city for our services over the past two years. The state and federal governments have grant money for law enforcement, which the city can use for a variety of reasons, including crime scene investigation. A lab is part of that package. I've researched the grants, called the state, and talked with Congressman Trent, and all that's needed is the paperwork filled out and the city manager to sign it. The people I've talked to say this whole process, once begun, can be completed in three to six months."

"How much time have you spent on this, Torres?"

"It's not important."

"Why is this important to you?"

She gave me a coy smile. "So, I can be closer to you." She winked. "I like what I do. The state's pay sucks. I need to make more money. And I've checked around.

CSI supervisor jobs don't grow on trees, and vacancies seldom occur."

"So, you want to create your own job?"

"You have a better idea?"

"No. I'm impressed."

"Are you pleased with the work I've done for the department?"

"Yes. Very. And Cahill is okay with this?"

"More than okay. He helped me put a business plan together and guided me all the way through the project. It lays out a systematic process. It's all in writing. All you have to do is get Jarret to approve it."

"Why is Cahill eager to help you?"

"I'm not supposed to tell you this; you can't give me away. There are rumors flying that Tallahassee wants to close our bureau and move everything to Orlando. That has been in the works for a while. If they do that, then there's a good chance I'll be out of a job, or worse, they'll bump me back to a tech position and make me commute to Orlando."

"Truth be told."

"Truth be told," said she.

"Are you prepared to present this to Jarret?"

"You mean stand up in front of people and sell this?"

"Of course. This is your proposal."

"I'd love it." A broad smile appeared on her face.

"I'll bet you would." I could see her holding a small group spellbound with her enthusiasm. "Will the rest of the techs from your unit come?"

"I can't promise that. If they shut the bureau down, then there would be no question. If not, Cahill would have a problem if I emptied the place out."

"Yeah, I wouldn't want you to do that."

When we arrived at the marina, an FDLE van was parked a few slips down from where the Hunts moored their boat. Torres' techs were packing equipment into the van.

We got out of my cruiser, and Torres asked the lead tech, "What do you have?"

"I have nothing. In fact, less than nothing."

"Explain."

"That boat hasn't moved in months, maybe longer. The batteries are missing, and the interior has enough dust on it to fill a borrow pit. The bilge pumps can't work without batteries, and there's water in the engine compartment. It would take a week or more to get this derelict in navigable condition. So, we have nothing."

I told Torres I'd get back to her on the crime lab and decided to drive out to Southeast Volusia Materials and talk with James Hunt again.

When I arrived at Hunt's office, he was in a meeting, and I had to wait fifteen minutes to see him. I thought about Torres' proposal and wished things hadn't jumped off the rails with Jarret. As I mulled options, it became clear how I might approach Jarret and prevent AJ from having to resign, and Alicia Torres was part of the solution.

When three men with white shirts and ties left Hunt's office, his assistant showed me in. It was obvious Hunt hadn't known I was there beforehand, and whatever mood he was in turned sour the moment I walked through the door.

"Chief McCain." The words came out like, *What in the hell are you doing here*?

"I just have a question or two, if you don't mind."

"I do mind."

I ignored him. "When you refused to pay McCoy the second blackmail installment, did you hear from her again?"

"No."

"You're an amazing liar, sir. I have copies of an email, confirmed by your wife, showing that when you refused to pay, McCoy offered you an out. Is any of this ringing a bell?"

"You mean about Pat? That she wanted me to fire him?"

"Why didn't you mention this the first time we talked?"

"You didn't ask me."

I wanted to get up and wipe the smirk off his face with the back of my hand. "Do you know why she wanted him fired?"

"No."

"Did you know then that she was Patrick McCoy's daughter?"

"No, not until you told me the other day."

"One more question. Did you tell Patrick McCoy about Ms. Rockwell's demand?"

"Look, Pat has been with me from the beginning. He's sober. He shows up every day. He does his job, and I never get complaints about him."

"The question was simple. Did you tell him about her demands?"

"Yes. I felt I owed it to him."

"Where is he now?"

"He's on a job, somewhere."

"Can you find him for me?"

Hunt picked up the phone on his desk, dialed a number and said, "Where's Pat McCoy right now?"

I could hear a voice on the other end but couldn't make out the words.

"Hold him. Find another driver to fill his remaining orders." Hunt put the phone down and said, "He just came in to refill his truck. Do you know where the dispatch building is?"

"Yes."

I walked out of the headquarters building and back to the parking lot. I called Downs.

"How is Martha doing?"

"She's asleep. At least I think she is. She's been locked away in my spare bedroom."

"I need you to get a warrant to search the home of Patrick McCoy. I need it now. I need you to check with the state and see if the McCoys own a boat. If they do, include it in the warrant. I want to search their home within the hour."

"I'll do my best."

"Call Torres and tell her I need her now."

"You have something?"

"Yes. Get working on the warrants."

29

When I pulled up to the dispatch office, Patrick McCoy was standing outside, waiting.

When he recognized the cruiser, he turned away from me and lifted his gaze to the cloudless sky. I slipped out of the car and met him by the entry door to the dispatch office.

"Mr. McCoy. You need to come with me, please."

"Why?"

"You haven't been straight with me."

"About what?"

"The fact that your daughter threatened you in the days before her death. The fact that she tried to blackmail your boss to get you fired."

McCoy shoved his hands into his pockets and looked at the toes of his shoes.

"Come with me, please."

I placed him in the back seat of the cruiser.

At the PD, I escorted him to a vacant interview room. I left the room, activated the recording equipment and reentered. By then he'd taken a seat. I sat opposite him.

McCoy wore a soiled ball cap with a Southeast Volusia Materials logo sewn on the front. His unkempt red hair curled up around the edges of his hat. His face, tanned and wrinkled from years in the sun, framed bloodshot green eyes. He hadn't shaved that morning. His hands, folded in front of him on the table, were dried and cracked from daily exposure to concrete.

I informed McCoy that we were recording our conversation and announced his name, my name, and the date and time. I advised him he was welcome to have an attorney present if he wished. He said nothing.

"Mr. McCoy, why was your daughter threatening you?"

"I told you before, my daughter was very sick."

"When she sent you the email saying you would pay for what you did to her, what was she accusing you of?"

"I told you already. She was accusing me of raping her."

"Were you aware she was blackmailing your boss to get you fired?"

"No."

"Mr. McCoy, I have a witness that will testify otherwise."

"All right, that little bitch was trying to destroy me."

"And she went to all the trouble to seduce and blackmail your boss because of an attempted rape that never happened? Did you tell your wife about your daughter's efforts to get you fired?"

"Yes."

"And what was her reaction?"

"We were both pretty upset."

"Do you own a boat, sir?"

"What does that have to do with this?"

"Just answer my question."

"Yes, a small fishing boat," McCoy confirmed.

"And where's the boat now?"

"At my house."

"Let's go back over the alleged rape. When did it occur?"

"When she was sixteen."

"You told me it happened when she was seventeen."

"Yes. I'm sorry, you're correct. It was when she wanted to buy a car, and she wanted me to give her the money."

"Your daughter was upset enough about you not having sex with her that she attempted to blackmail you and get you fired from your job?"

"You have no idea what my daughter was like."

"I'm getting ready to execute a search warrant of your home and boat," I said. "I'm certain I'll find evidence you murdered your daughter, Mr. McCoy."

"I swear I didn't kill her."

"I'll tell you what I think, Mr. McCoy. I think you had sex with your daughter. Given the level of anger and rage she exhibited, I think you were having sex with your daughter for a long time. Now, from where I stand, that's the only reasonable explanation. Does your wife know about any of this?"

McCoy was silent.

"Please stand up, sir. I'm placing you under arrest for the murder of your daughter."

"All right, all right. I was having sex with her, but I swear to you, I didn't kill her."

"And when did you first initiate sex with your daughter?"

"When she was eleven. You've no idea how beautiful she was."

"And how long did you continue to have sex with her?"

"Until she left home."

"For six years, you raped your daughter?"

He dropped his head and said nothing.

"Does your wife know of any of this?"

"No."

"When you told her about your daughter trying to get you fired, how did you explain it to her? That she was still trying to get even with you for not having sex with her to buy a car?"

He said nothing.

"Where were you on Sunday night between ten p.m. and five the next morning?"

"I was home. Asleep."

"At ten o'clock at night?"

"I go to bed before eight. I have to be at the plant by five in the morning."

"And your wife will testify to that?"

"Yes."

"I'm going to place you in a holding cell until I finish searching your home and boat."

I stood up. While he sat there, I looked down at him and said, "I find it hard to believe you had the balls to accuse your daughter of being sick and to blame her for trying to repay you for what you did to her. You're one sick bastard, McCoy. Wait here. An officer will escort you to a cell."

When I walked out of the interview room, Torres was waiting for me in my office. I gave Torres the address of the McCoy home.

30

The yard at the McCoy house was overgrown, and no one had mowed it in months. The home was a low single-story home with a bougainvillea vine overgrowing a single-car carport. Torres and her team pulled their van in behind me onto a gravel drive filled with weeds. We parked behind an older white Honda sedan. To the left of the home was a trailered small boat haphazardly covered with a beige tarp. I waited to approach the house until Torres and her people unloaded their equipment from the van.

Verna McCoy answered the door, still dressed in her pajamas. She was tying a knot on her bathrobe and straightening her hair with her hand.

"Mrs. McCoy, we've a warrant to search your home and to examine your boat. May we come in?"

"Would you mind explaining why?"

"Could you step out of the house, please." There was a small porch large enough for two lawn chairs. "Why don't you and I sit while my folks do their work?"

"You still haven't explained what you're doing." She eased herself into the nearest chair.

I inched past her and sat in the other. "I have your husband in custody. We're questioning him regarding your daughter's murder. Were you aware your daughter was blackmailing James Hunt to get your husband fired from his job?"

"Yes, Pat told me. But my husband could never do anything like that."

"Were you aware your daughter attempted to blackmail your husband a couple of years ago? She accused him of raping her."

"I just found out about it when he told me she was trying to get him fired from his job."

"Was you husband home on Sunday night between ten and twelve p.m.?"

"Yes, he was home."

"Were you aware your husband was having sex with your daughter?"

"That's not possible."

"According to your husband, he began having sex with your daughter when she was eleven and continued until she moved out of the house."

"That's just not possible," she repeated.

"Mrs. McCoy, I have his statement on tape. I just came from my interview with him."

Alicia Torres appeared at the front door. She said, "I need a moment."

I asked Mrs. McCoy to remain where she was and followed Torres into the house.

"I found apricot and seeds in the refrigerator and chemicals in the shed in the back yard to make a crude home version of cyanide. Apricot seeds, by themselves, don't contain the harmful version of cyanide, hydrogen cyanide. However, they contain amygdalin, which you can metabolize into hydrogen cyanide. The chemicals I found in the shed can be used in the various steps to refine it. I haven't found any cyanide per se, but everything needed to make it is here."

"Have your folks gone over the boat?"

"They found a pair of women's flip-flops. If there are epithelial cells on them, we can match them to the victim.

We're still not done. I think they're dusting the boat for prints now."

I went back out to the porch and sat with a tearful Verna McCoy.

I said, "We've found the materials in your home to make cyanide, Mrs. McCoy. When we lift the prints from the fruit and chemicals, we will have enough to convict your husband of murder."

"That poor girl," she sobbed. "I had no idea. She never said a word to me. Not a word." Tears streamed down her face. "And you said he kept having sex with her until she moved out?"

"That's what he told me."

"Oh, God. I've made a horrible mistake. It never dawned on me it could be true, but now it makes sense."

"What mistake, Mrs. McCoy?"

"I killed my daughter. She was going to destroy us. I couldn't let that happen. Now I understand why. What have I done?"

"Start from the beginning, Mrs. McCoy."

"Eleven. That's when it all began. That's when she started acting out. That's when all of her problems began. God help me."

"Please, tell me how this happened."

"When Patrick received that threatening email, and Jim Hunt told Patrick about her seducing him and blackmailing him to fire Pat, I believed she'd gone off the deep end."

"Why didn't you call the police?"

"You didn't know our daughter. She was vicious. Her accusations, even if they'd been false, would have destroyed Patrick. They'd have ruined us both. I called Sally and asked her to come see me. I had gone on the internet and learned how to make cyanide and bought the chemicals and equipment to do it. She came to the house after dinner, and I offered her a margarita—that's her favorite drink—and poured the mixture I had made into it. James had already gone to sleep, and she was dead within a few moments."

Verna cried now in earnest. She kept repeating, "What've I done?"

"After she was dead, what did you do next?"

"I woke up Patrick. He'd no idea I had planned this. Now I wish I had killed him instead."

"Mrs. McCoy..."

"It was my idea to take her out to Disappearing Island. When she was eight or nine, we used to take the boat out there every weekend to swim and have a picnic. This is the only place I could think of where at one point we were all happy. From there, I thought the tide would take her out of Ponce Inlet and out to sea."

"So, your husband helped?"

"I couldn't lift her myself, and I couldn't have managed the boat without his help."

Torres appeared at the front door. "We're finished with the house and boat."

"Were finished here, too." I said to Mrs. McCoy, "I'm placing you under arrest for the murder of Sally McCoy." I Mirandized her.

Torres packed up the scene, I placed Mrs. McCoy in the cruiser, and we returned to the PD.

31

After I installed Mrs. McCoy in a holding cell, I called Downs and asked her to fill out all the charging papers and coordinate them with the assistant state's attorney. I drove to Downs' small home and once inside it was clear from cups on the coffee table that her and Martha Johnson had been engaged in conversation. I pulled a kitchen chair into the living room and sat in it backwards. Downs said she would head to the PD to complete the paperwork on the McCoys.

I stood, walked across to the couch where Johnson was sitting, bent down and hugged her, then joined her on the couch. Downs left for the PD.

Johnson said, "They called a bit ago. Hunter did the autopsy and is ready to release the body."

"This has to be hard, Martha. Can I do anything? I want to help if I can."

"Chief Downs and Leslie have taken a collection at both PDs for Deshon and raised enough for a simple casket and a plot at the same cemetery where the two slain Daytona Beach officers will be buried. Chief Downs wants Deshon included with the two officers in the funeral procession to the cemetery with full police escort. Then I'll have a small graveside service for Deshon separate from theirs. I thought it was very kind of him to do that."

And classy, I thought. "Martha, I want you to take as much time off as you feel you need."

"I was going to talk to you about that. I know this will put you in a bind, but I need to take a leave of absence. I have family in Chicago. I thought I'd go there and try to make sense of all this before I figure out what I'm going to do."

"Leave isn't a problem."

"I may not be coming back, Chief."

"Then again, you might. You don't need to decide now. Take your time."

She talked about the details of the funeral and thoughts she'd had about the service. She asked me about the McCoy case, and I went through the highlights with her, but within a few moments, her mind was elsewhere. I didn't think she heard much of my summary. She said she was fine, that she had much to do. She said she knew I was busy and, in a polite way, let me know she was ready for me to leave.

We both stood, I hugged her and as I turned to move to the front door, she said, "I should have never let that boy agree to testify, Jed. Never."

"You did what you thought was right. Don't be hard on yourself." The words were hollow, and I knew it. It would be a long time before she forgave herself, if ever.

32

Jim Cahill called me on my way into the PD. He said he was in my office, waiting on me, and needed to talk.

At my office, Cahill was sitting in my chair, talking with one of his special agents on his cellphone. He started to get up, but I gestured for him to remain and sat in one of the guest chairs.

He finished his call and said, "Torres called me and said you arrested Verna McCoy."

"All the way through this case, I've been thinking there had to be a better explanation for Sally McCoy's reckless behavior than her being an evil seed or having a mental illness. It's as though all the men she blackmailed and tried to harm were substitutes for an abusive father. She was crying out for help, and no one was listening."

"And the mother, for God's sakes!"

"She was in complete denial, as mothers often are in cases of incest."

"The father participated in the murder?"

"After the fact. The assistant state's attorney will charge them both. I'm hoping they will also charge Patrick McCoy with the sexual abuse of his daughter."

Cahill asked, "How's Martha Johnson? I can't imagine being in her shoes today."

"I just left her, Jim. She's raw, but she has funeral arrangements to make and a boy to bury. She told me she wants a leave of absence. She said she may not be back."

"What'll she do?"

"I hope she stays. She's an excellent officer. She is, however, well-educated with management experience and won't have trouble finding work if she decides to leave. Did you want to talk to me about something?"

"Jarret called me and asked me to meet with him. That's why I'm here."

"What did he want?"

"A sounding board. When AJ McFarland resigned, Jarret began to consider he'd acted too hastily. He wanted to talk about the crime lab, and I filled him in on the study Torres had done."

"I understand you helped her with it."

"I didn't do much. She just needed a little guidance, that's all. He asked me if I thought his demand for a rigid chain of command was reasonable. I told him I thought it was."

"But?"

"I told him I thought you'd followed it. That what happened with the crime lab issue was happenstance and not an effort on your part to go around him. I also said I thought you; the mayor and he all wanted the same thing and his demand for you to sever your relationship with McFarland was extreme. He asked me for some advice and how to work this out."

"What advice did you give him?"

"He asked me not to share that with you. I have the feeling he's reached a decision, and he'll act on it soon."

"That was it?"

"No. I told Jarret there was an excellent possibility the FDLE would close the bureau in Daytona. This is confidential. I told him time was of the essence and if he didn't act on the crime lab, these folks would be moved to other parts of the state or quit and find jobs elsewhere."

"So, when will this happen?"

"Soon. I've already been told I'm to replace the SAC in the Orlando bureau."

"A promotion?"

"Yeah, I'll get a little more money. A lot more responsibility, though. It's a good thing Sandy is VP of publicity at NASCAR, or we would be struggling."

"Are you moving to Orlando?"

"No, I'm going to commute. I still have unfinished work in Volusia and Flagler counties that will take time to clear up. Besides, there's no way Sandy will leave Daytona."

"This is the second time you've been called upon to save my job, Jim."

"You're a good cop, Jed. They're lucky to have you, but you're still not out of the woods."

"Open the bottom right-hand drawer."

He bent over, slid the drawer open and produced a half-full bottle of Jim Beam and two shot glasses. He opened the bottle, filled the glasses with the golden liquid, reached over the desk and handed one to me.

I held up my glass. "To staying out of the woods."

We both drank.

Cahill said, "If you're good at this job, the woods are always nearby. If they aren't, you're not aggressive enough."

"Personal experience?"

"It comes with the job, Jed."

33

That afternoon, Ashley Rand called and asked me over to her place for dinner. I took off early, went home and cleaned up. I drove over the South Causeway Bridge, doubled back to Riverside Drive and parked in front of the Rand home at six-thirty.

Ashley met me at the door. She had her hair down and wore a sleeveless white blouse, white tight-fitting jeans and sandals. The house smelled of something Italian, and she smelled of perfume.

When I walked inside the house, I could see from the expression on her face that dinner was the last thing on her mind.

I said, "You look..." but I didn't say another word before she was in my arms.

I said to myself, *So much for going slow.*

After she reheated dinner, which was excellent, Ashley packed a small ice chest with a pitcher of margaritas and two glasses, which we carried across the street to her dock on the Indian River. With an upper deck over a motorized boatlift, her dock put my simple dock to shame. We climbed the stairs to the deck and sat in two Adirondack chairs with a small teak cocktail table between. She opened the cooler, poured two drinks and handed one to me.

She said, "To many more evenings as delicious as this one."

I touched my glass to hers. "I'll toast to that. Delicious is such an interesting choice of words."

"Well, you've had a busy day, Chief."

I had filled her in on the arrest of the McCoys. "I guess we're finished with Belford. I hate to let the guy off the hook, but without his initial input, the case would have moved more slowly. You can tell him to live his life."

"Despite all the moving parts to Sally McCoy's life, Trent was in love with her."

I said, "While it first appeared everyone had motive to kill her, both Trent and Belford found something redeeming in her. It was odd that both men knew all the horrible truths about her yet still loved her."

"I just don't understand how a mother could have killed her own child."

"Patrick McCoy had Verna convinced that their daughter was mentally ill and capable of unbound evil. As Sally's demands increased, he convinced his wife their daughter's out-of-control behavior stemmed from sociopathic tendencies. When the girl threatened to take away Patrick's job, I believe Verna saw this as a struggle between good and evil. She was protecting her husband by taking her daughter's life. She didn't know about the incest. Despite this, she took the life of her daughter with premeditation."

"How old was Sally when her father began to abuse her?"

"Eleven."

"My daughter Nicole is just two years older. What a horrible thing to happen to a young girl."

"At eleven, a child is knitting together all their sexual wiring, and to be raped by a parent... No wonder she was screwed up. Her whole life points to getting even with her father for what he did to her."

"Do you have children?"

"No," I said. "My ex didn't want children."

"And you?"

"Yes. I'm very open to that. Where's your daughter tonight?"

"She's with Eddy."

"I'd like to meet her."

"It pleases me you do, Jed. Despite what happened tonight, for her sake, I want to take it slow."

"I'm good with that."

"Anything more on you losing your job?" Ashley asked.

"You mean am I any closer to being a deadbeat ex-cop?"

"I drove by your house today. It looks like you're just one step away from being homeless." She smiled. "You need a good income to fix that place up."

"Ah, now don't you start on me, too. I get daily grief from AJ about it. Jim Cahill met with Neil Jarret, and since AJ resigned as mayor, Jarret has been having second thoughts about my dismissal. Cahill thinks Jarret is trying to find a face-saving way to walk back the firing."

"That sounds promising. You sure you don't need me to be your agent?"

"Jarret wouldn't stand a chance against you, so I think I'll hold you in reserve."

"You're such a diplomat." She paused, then said, "You'll work it out."

"So far, I haven't done anything. It seems to be working out."

"Good."

"You wouldn't go out with me if I was a homeless retired ex-NYPD cop?"

"You need to do something with that house of yours. It needs a woman's touch."

"It needs more than that; it needs a bulldozer's touch. What'll happen to this house? Will you keep it?"

"I'm not sure. Eddy is willing to give up the house or keep it if I don't want it. It is up to me. The taxes are horrendous, and it's a lot to take care of, but Nicole grew up in this house. I'm trying to feel her out on it. Eddy and I are on the same page that we want to minimize the impact of our divorce on her."

"When will it be final?"

"It is already. I guess we should have worked out all the property issues before we signed the papers, but I trust Eddy to be fair, and until now, he has been. Nicole is the reason we've taken our time."

"Can I ask you a question?"

She nodded.

"Are you still in love with your husband?"

"I loved him. I still care for him. But no, I'm not. What occurred earlier tonight would never have happened if I did."

The breeze from the south across the deck was balmy. The sky was ablaze with stars. As the evening progressed in comfortable conversation, we both engaged in the give and take of finding out about each other. Ashley made me feel comfortable enough to be wide open to her. I know she felt the same with me. Despite my job status still hanging in the air, sitting on the deck with her that night was the first time since I had arrived in Coronado Beach that I felt my future was secure—that I belonged.

Epilogue

Patrick McCoy pleaded guilty to accessory to murder after the fact and received the maximum sentence of fifteen years. He also pleaded guilty to the sexual molestation of his daughter and received a twenty-five-year sentence without parole added to his accessory sentence. Verna McCoy pleaded guilty to first-degree murder, and the judge sentenced her to life in prison.

When confronted with the evidence from Sally McCoy's ledger, Demarcus Brown agreed to testify against his Colombian-sponsored supplier in exchange for a light sentence on state drug trafficking charges. Brown received a five-year sentence in Florida State Prison at Raiford. His supplier was awaiting trial on federal charges for smuggling and distributing across state lines.

Three members of the Evil City Boys who murdered Deshon Johnson and the two police officers were tried as adults and convicted of first-degree murder with special circumstances. Those same juveniles were also charged and convicted of second-degree murder in the beating death of Charley Grant.

The other nine juvenile gang members who stood by and watched the fatal beating of Grant and did nothing, were charged as adults with manslaughter. Although they were offered reduced sentences in exchange for testimony against the gang's leaders, Deshon's death was a still fresh memory on what happens to those who would testify against the gang.

Police departments across the state sent representatives to escort the caskets of Deshon Johnson and the two slain police officers from the funeral home across town to the cemetery. The procession of police cruisers and motorcycles was a mile and a half long. At the cemetery, the Johnson party split away to a separate section of the cemetery, where all officers of the Coronado Beach Police Department provided Martha Johnson's son full military honors.

In addition to the police department and city employees attending, it surprised me to see how large Martha Johnson's family was and the number of friends, both Black and White, who came to support her.

Once the pastor gave the eulogy, Martha Johnson stood and spoke of her son in laudatory terms and railed against gang activity. She stressed the importance of a father's influence in the life of boys growing into manhood. She spoke of the need to eradicate racism in all its forms and blamed it as the fertile soil for the growth of the gang that had attracted her son.

Following the funeral, Martha Johnson took a leave of absence. Despite her warnings that she might not come back, two weeks after the funeral, she called me to let me know she would be returning.

AJ McFarland, Neil Jarret and I met in Jarret's office to discuss my dismissal and AJ's resignation. Jarret spent twenty minutes explaining the difficulties he'd experienced when Chief Grizzle had conducted business with the council, ignoring chain of command and Jarret's authority. AJ said he would withdraw his resignation if I were to remain as chief. He said he hadn't been aware of Jarret's sensitivity in that area and thought he was helping. AJ promised that while he may discuss matters related to the city with me, he would never again bring a

PD matter before the council without first consulting Jarret. I did the same. Jarret withdrew my dismissal, and AJ rescinded his resignation.

Alicia Torres, at Jarret's request, presented her crime lab study to him first and then to the city council. The council approved the project and gave the city manager authority to add the positions needed. I hired Torres and her entire staff the day after the FDLE announced the shuttering of the Daytona bureau. I gave Torres the rank of lieutenant and a pay raise. I promoted Downs to commander, and I gave her responsibility for supervising investigations and Torres. Jim Cahill assumed special agent in charge duties in Orlando, and Coronado Beach remained within his jurisdiction. The move to a larger office came with a small raise, he told me, but "ain't no one getting rich here."

-End-

Following the Preview of Firestorm, there is information about all the other Novels by Bill Cronin

Preview of Third Novel
In the Jed McCain Mysteries

Firestorm

Firestorm 1

"He's been missing for three days, Chief McCain."

The woman sitting across from me was attractive, in her late thirties. She had tied her medium brown hair into a ponytail and wore gym shorts, a tank top and bright lime green running shoes—athletic clothing a jogger might wear.

I opened the pencil drawer in my desk and removed a ballpoint pen. "What's his name?"

"Sebastian. Sebastian Sabatini."

I picked up a yellow legal pad, placed it on the blotter and printed his name on the first line. "Your name?"

"Katherine Grant."

"Your relationship to Mr. Sabatini?"

"I guess you'd describe me as his girlfriend." She sat perched on the edge of her chair, trying to read what I was writing on the pad. Her ponytail hung across her left shoulder and down her chest.

"You sound a little unsure of your relationship."

"That's because I've never been sure. But he calls me every day, and I haven't heard from him in three days."

"Does he live with you?"

"No, not regularly."

"What makes you so sure he's missing?"

"Aside from what I just told you, that he hasn't called me," she said with irritation, "I've gone by where he stays, and his car was there and, well, things didn't look right. There was no sign of him."

"Things didn't look right?"

"His car door was wide open, the keys were in the ignition, and his cellphones were lying on the passenger seat. My guess is that the car had been sitting for a while."

"What made you think that?" I asked.

"The battery was dead, probably from the open door."

"You say 'the place where he's staying' as though it's temporary."

"Sebastian is odd, Chief McCain. He refers to himself as a minimalist. That's his fancy name for a freeloader."

"You mean he's homeless?"

"Not homeless, exactly. He defines home on a day-by-day basis. He takes advantage of people's generosity. For example, take the two-acre place he's staying at now. He did investigative work for the woman who lives there in exchange for a place to park his travel trailer for a time. Once he finished his work, they agreed he'd move on. Only Sebastian wouldn't leave, and he forced her to evict him legally."

"I'm reading between the lines, but it sounds like this isn't the first time this has happened."

"No. It isn't. People have tried to help him, and he took advantage... No, that's not strong enough. He returned their generosity with abuse."

"Yet he's your boyfriend."

"Sebastian is a complex person, Chief. There are several sides to him. He can be charming and endearing. We built our relationship on that side of him; that's the part I fell in love with. He can also be difficult—exceedingly difficult—the reason I put limits on our relationship."

"What do you mean by difficult?" I asked.

"He has a violent temper. He's mean-spirited when he doesn't get his way. He seems to thrive on confrontation."

"Was he ever violent with you?"

"You mean did he ever hit me? No. He lost his temper with me several times, and I sent him packing. For some reason, he didn't retaliate."

"He did with others?"

"Yes."

"Do you think his disappearance is connected to the violent side of him?"

"Very much so. Something has happened to him."

"Have you considered your boyfriend left of his own accord? What if he doesn't want us to find him?"

"I don't think so."

"What makes you so sure?" I asked, tapping the pen on the desk blotter.

"He's a little agoraphobic as far as this area is concerned. His family is from New York, but he sees them infrequently. I've tried to get him to travel, but he's unwilling to leave his 'home,' as he calls it. Even though he has no home to speak of, the thought of him going somewhere else creates anxiety for him."

"You said your boyfriend was doing investigative work?"

"He's a licensed private investigator." Ms. Grant pulled out a picture from a small quilted handbag that hung across her shoulder and handed it to me. "I took this picture with my phone and printed it, so it is a little grainy."

Sabatini had a dark complexion and could have passed for someone from the Middle East. He was leaning against the driver's side door of a car with his arms folded over his chest. He hadn't shaved nor combed his thinning black hair and looked as if he'd just woken. Judging by his height in relationship to the car, he was over six feet tall, in his mid to late thirties and muscular. Wrinkled jeans, a T-shirt and soiled running shoes completed his unkempt appearance. His face was thin and angular, mouth small, nose long and thin, ears close to his head, and black eyebrows hung low over his eyes.

Ms. Grant leaned forward in her chair to look at the picture. "He doesn't look like much in that picture, but Seby—that's my name for him—is intelligent and engaging, when he wants to be."

I took a card out of the pencil drawer and handed it to her. "Could you text the picture to me? My cellphone number is on the bottom of the card."

Ms. Grant tapped the screen on her phone. "There, I sent it to you."

"What else can you tell me about him?"

"Sebastian is a private, secretive person. He talks about himself sparingly and changed the subject when I asked probing questions about his past, except when he ranted about his ex, or the people he felt were trying to hurt him."

"Ex?" I asked. "He was married?"

"Ex-girlfriend. Sebastian would never marry anyone. You should speak with her. He lived with her for six years."

"Do you think she might have had something to do with his disappearance?"

"I have no idea. I've only spoken to her once when Sebastian and I started dating."

"And?"

"She warned me about him. She specifically said that I shouldn't let him move in with me. She said that I'd regret it."

"Did you...let him move in?"

"No. He'd spend the night with me from time to time, but no, I didn't let him move in. I wasn't looking for a full-time companion. I've had two spectacularly awful marriages, Chief. I was not in the market for another. I like my independence."

"Do you have the ex's name?"

"Jane Frost." She reached into her purse and pulled out two pieces of paper. "Here is Jane's information."

I looked at the first piece of paper with a handwritten address on it. Her residence was on beachside, off Flagler Avenue. The city of Coronado Beach was divided by the Indian River. Locals referred to the part of town west of the river as mainland and the barrier island east of the river as beachside.

"She works in Daytona somewhere, at an attorney's office, I think. I don't know where." Ms. Grant handed me the second piece of paper. "This is the address and phone number of his parents. They live in Beacon, New York."

Beacon was up the Hudson River from New York City. I'd been there on business with the NYPD.

I asked, "Have you contacted them?"

"Yes. I reached out to them to see if they'd heard from him. I learned that he called his father every day. When his father told me he hadn't heard from Sebastian either, I decided to come to you. They're on their way down now. They're worried sick."

"Why me? Why didn't you call 911?"

"Ashley... I mean Ms. Rand suggested I come to see you. I work in her office as a paralegal. She suggested that if I spoke to you, it might have a higher priority."

Ashley Rand was an attorney in Coronado Beach whom I'd been seeing for the last seven months. I looked down at my notes.

"You said Sabatini has a violent temper and that he is confrontational."

"He thrives on confrontation, Chief McCain."

"Do any names come to mind of people who would want to harm him?"

"Every day he told me about this person or that he'd gone off on. There were so many, I hardly paid attention. One incident, over a year ago, that I do remember had to do with your police department. One of your patrol officers pulled him over for a minor infraction. Sebastian claimed that your officer assaulted him and put him in jail. When they released him, he filed a complaint with the department and one with the Florida Department of Law Enforcement. I also remember bailiffs escorting him out of the clerk of court's office in Deland after a belligerent confrontation he had with the clerk over a restraining order he'd filed against someone. He was fearless. He angered scores of people, Chief."

"And you think he took on the wrong person?"

"Yes."

"You found his car. Where was he staying?"

"On a piece of property on the edge of town." She gave me the address.

"Did you touch the cellphones you said you found in the car?"

"No. I didn't touch anything, except to close the door of his car."

"We will need to get your fingerprints," I said.

"I understand."

"You said you found two phones?"

"Yes. I didn't know that he had two."

"And you say he had a trailer on the property?"

"Yes, one that hitches to the bumper of a car. A small one."

"Did you have a key?"

"No. I've never been in it. I've only been out there twice. Once when we were going out somewhere and he forgot his wallet, and the second time when I found his abandoned car."

I looked at my notes, which had filled two pages on my legal pad. "All right. I'll have more questions, but this should get me started."

"Behind all the bluster and anger, I've never seen him hurt anyone. He could throw a tantrum, and he could be mean, but I don't think he'd physically hurt anyone unless someone tried to hurt him."

I stood, and so did Ms. Grant. She extended her hand, and I shook it.

"Thanks, Chief McCain."

"I'll be in touch when I've something to report." As she turned to leave, I said, "One more thing."

She turned and faced me.

"How did you and Sabatini meet?"

"He does investigative work for our law firm from time to time."

"Ashley Rand's firm?"

"Yes. But it was her ex-husband, Eddy, who hired him. Ashley, I mean Ms. Rand, rarely gets involved in criminal cases."

Firestorm 2

Sergeant Martha Johnson, my assistant, found the empty chair just vacated by Katherine Grant in my office. Six months ago, her only son Deshon had become ensnared in a city-boy gang in Daytona. He had been due to testify against the gang who had beaten an elderly man to death as part of a gang initiation. Three gang members had gunned down Deshon and two Daytona Beach police officers in a safe house before he could testify.

Johnson had returned from leave following her son's death. While she continued to run the department and executed her considerable responsibilities with professionalism, I knew a part of her had died when the gang had taken her son's life. She'd encouraged Deshon to "do the right thing" and testify. Now she blamed herself for his death, and no amount of persuasion could extract her from that hell. At just over five feet tall, Johnson had lost sixty pounds and looked gaunt, her uniform nearly sagging on her, and she appeared older than her years. I missed the Johnson who would stand at the door to my office, hands on her ample hips, and chew my ass for some small infraction of protocol, or tell me I could kiss her ass if I asked her to get me coffee or requested something from her she felt was beneath her dignity. My heart bled for her.

"I heard that woman mention Sebastian Sabatini," she said.

"You heard that from your cubicle."

"I'm the assistant to the chief. Nothing gets past me."

"Apparently not."

"The department has a long history with Mr. Sabatini, Chief. Before you go a step further, you should talk to Carl Stanton. He nearly lost his job over Sabatini."

"All right. Ms. Grant just asked me to open a missing person case on Sabatini. He's disappeared."

"Good riddance as far as the department is concerned. The FDLE was up Grizzle's ass on that one."

"What happened?"

"Following two months of investigation, FDLE didn't find anything that substantiated Sabatini's claim, and the city dropped the matter. However, Grizzle was under pressure to fire Stanton and his partner, and Mr. Jarret was having a fit over it. Mr. Jarret didn't think much of our chief then."

"Would you find Commander Downs for me?" I asked.

Johnson pointed behind me to the phone on my credenza, stood up from her seat and left my office. At least she didn't totally ignore me. It wasn't a "kiss my ass," but it was close. A good sign she was on the mend.

Commander Leslie Downs, head of the investigations division of the department, which included a squad of detectives and crime scene investigators, was tall, slender and athletically built. Her cubicle was in a corner on the second floor of the PD, wedged in by a dozen or more empty military surplus desks crammed together into a bullpen for her detectives. Downs was on the phone when I rounded the corner to her cube. She held up her index finger and hurried the conversation she was having, then hung up.

"What's up?" She spun around in her chair to face me, and she instantly saw my reaction to her haircut. Downs had had long light red hair that hung to the middle of her back. Now it was short with pointed sideburns, and the cut tapered at the neck. "I got tired of messing with it," she said.

The week before, during an arrest, a perp had grabbed her by her hair and nearly got the best of her.

I handed her the piece of paper with the address where Sabatini had been living that Ms. Grant had given me. "His girlfriend reported him missing. I need a warrant to search his car and a travel trailer he owns parked at that address."

"You sure you want to do this? You know who this guy is, don't you?"

"No, but obviously everyone else does."

"Sabatini isn't worth the department's time or trouble. You execute a search warrant on his property, and I guarantee you he'll sue you and me and anyone else connected to it. I'm not even sure I can find a judge who'll stick his neck out and issue one."

"All the more reason to have a search warrant. Do your best."

Even though major cases came under Downs' responsibilities, she and I worked on those cases together as partners. It was not that Downs was incapable. She was an excellent investigator. I had grudgingly accepted the position of chief, but in truth, I loved detective work. Fortunately, Downs and I made a good team, and she enjoyed the camaraderie as much as I did.

"When do you want to execute the warrant?" she asked.

"ASAP. I have Officer Stanton coming into the PD now."

"You picked the right guy. He'll give you an earful." She tried to flip her non-existent long hair over her shoulder, caught herself and said, "This will take some getting used to." She smiled.

"It looks good," I lied. "Call me when you're ready to roll."

Six-foot two-inch Sergeant Carl Stanton stood at attention and filled the doorway to my office. I motioned for him to grab a chair.

Once he sat down, I said, "Relax. Everything is fine. I just need background on a reported missing person." Stanton had the body of a weightlifter. With his blond crew cut and smooth face, he looked ten years younger than his thirty-nine years. He'd been an MP in the Marine Corps, retired after 20 years, completed the police academy and been hired on here three years ago as a police officer.

"Sabatini," he said, as one might invoke the name of the devil.

"Yes. Fill me in."

"My partner and I were on patrol and observed a car with an expired tag. We pulled the car over, got out of the cruiser, and I asked the driver for his license. The guy, Sabatini, said, 'I'm not giving you a fucking thing. I haven't done anything wrong.'

"I explained to him that he had an expired tag, and before I could finish explaining why we'd stopped him, he bolted from the car and tried to hit me with his car door. Then he goes into this rage, asking, 'don't you have anything better to do than harass people over petty bullshit?' I again asked him for his license, and I told him to get back into his car.

"Then he flies into a rage again, screaming at us that he was going to file a complaint and that we'd be sorry we'd ever pulled him over, that we'd no idea who we were messing with. He became so aggressive, I ordered him back into his car or we'd cuff him. It was then that he shoved me, and it took both my partner and me to restrain him. I cuffed him, put him in the back of the cruiser, had his car towed to an impound yard, and charged him with assaulting a police officer. On the way to the station, he was screaming continuously, calling us every expletive you can imagine. We added 'resisting' to the charges.

"Then the shit hit the fan when we placed him in a holding cell. He was yelling that I'd assaulted him. That we'd yanked him out of the car and brutally cuffed him because he'd asked why we stopped him. He demanded to talk to the chief and screamed that we were violating his rights. He said he was going to sue the department and me personally.

"We called Grizzle just to get the guy to shut up. That was a huge mistake. All Sabatini had to say was that he was going to sue Grizzle, and Grizzle let him go. He didn't even listen to what we had to say. He just let him go. He even apologized to that bastard. Can you believe it?

"Then Sabatini files a complaint anyway with the department and the FDLE that I assaulted him. Grizzle suspended me and my partner without pay for two months until he could 'resolve the matter.' Grizzle had the city manager convinced that we'd overreacted. It wasn't until Jim Cahill with the FDLE interviewed my partner and me separately that he confirmed that Sabatini had an expired tag. He interviewed Sabatini himself and concluded that we were telling the truth and that it was Sabatini who'd in fact assaulted us. Grizzle restored us to duty but never paid us back pay or apologized. By then, the chief was unwilling to go after Sabatini, preferring to 'let sleeping dogs lie.'"

I said, "From listening to people in the department, it sounds like we've had multiple run-ins with him."

"I had another run-in with him two months after the PD put me back on duty. A retired female police officer from Orlando PD lives on beachside and called 911 about a suspicious vehicle parked in the alley behind her house. She lived alone and was concerned for her safety. When we rolled up into the alley, I recognized Sabatini's car. When I turned the spotlight on, Sabatini got out of his car, hopping mad. I got out of the cruiser and made sure he didn't get within ten feet of me. I asked him what he was doing in the alley and told him we had a complaint about him.

"He said it was none of our effing business. That it was a public alley and he'd every right to park in it. I told him that while that may be true, we'd every right to remain there with him. I turned on the blue lights, and we waited him out. After five minutes or so, he got back in the car, stuck his arm out the window, flipped me the bird and drove off. I didn't learn until later that he was stalking his ex-girlfriend, who lived five houses down from where he parked."

"Stalking his ex?"

"All the info I can give you is incomplete. His ex-girlfriend sent him packing, and he didn't take her throwing him out very well. He set up a camp behind a vacant house next door and harassed her. She filed a restraining order, and dispatch sent us to her house multiple times to deal with him. Grizzle was afraid of him and never let us do anything more than enforce the order to the letter."

"Was he ever arrested?"

"No. Like I said, Grizzle was afraid of him. You need to talk to the ex. She'll give you an earful."

"Is that it?"

"No. Sabatini careened from one interpersonal disaster to another. The slightest affront would ignite him; a take-no-prisoners situation would erupt. He was on fire, Chief, and burned everyone around him. Every officer in the department has crossed paths with him over the last two or three years."

"Anyone stand out that would want to do him harm?"

Stanton raised an eyebrow. "You're serious? If he is missing, my guess is he messed with the wrong person. Good luck with finding that person. The list of suspects would go around the block. I'd start with the ex. Sabatini put her through hell."

Contact Information

To receive updates and news on Bill Cronin's books,
"like" his Facebook page.
http://facebook.com/billcroninwrite.
You can contact the author directly:
billcroninwrite@gmail.com

Bill Cronin's Other Books

Stand-Alone Novels
Available as e-books.
Dial Tone, 2012
The Tainted Lady, 2014

Jack McNamara Chronicles
All available as e-books and
paperback.
The Song of the Mockingbird, Book 1, 2013
Ruby's Story, Book 2, 2014
Letting Go, Book 3, 2015
Joe and the Governor, Book 4, 2016

Jed McCain Mysteries
All available as e-books, audiobooks and
paperback.
Night Fire, Book 1, 2017
Playing with Fire, Book 2, 2017
Firestorm, Book 3, 2025